MILK & CROAKIES

SAM CHEEVER

ELECTRIC PROSE PUBLICATIONS

Farmer Blue has lost his cows and doesn't know where to find them. But Farmer blue has found guess who, to wrangle the magic that hides them.

I'm really not much of a country mouse. Up until recently, my idea of the great outdoors has been Enchanted Park in the center of the city. But my job is to wrangle magical artifacts. So, when a local farmer calls to tell me his dairy cows are disappearing and he thinks it's the work of a rogue artifact...sigh...it appears I'm about to get a crash course in becoming a farm girl.

These cows haven't just meandered away chewing their cuds. They've actually disappeared.

Poof!

As in here one minute, gone the next. Which means it's up to me to don tall rubber boots and traverse the cow bumps...slog through the cow patties...and reach into the abyss to try to drag them back.

I'm not sure how the frog and the cat are going to help with this one. I really didn't want to bring them along at all. But you know how insistent they can be...

Wait...where's the frog? Has anybody seen my cat?

Slimy! Wicked! Where on earth have you gone?

Poof?

IN SEARCH OF A LARGE, NAKED
FEMALE WEARING A BELL

"*I*nside the tank of the Magic Muffin Maker," I told the little hobgoblin standing happily before me. With that pronouncement, Hobs' oversized ears drooped and took his smile with them.

"Horse halitosis," Hobs murmured.

I took up the smile he'd lost. "You can't beat me at this game, Hobs. I'm the queen of my domain."

Okay, maybe I was being a little cocky, but ever since I'd formally bonded with Croakies and the artifact library, I was a walking treasure map for everything inside the place.

Well, everything magical, anyway. I still couldn't find my car keys from that morning. I could swear I'd put them into my jacket pocket when I got back from the grocery.

"Jack's bag of magic beans," Sebille said.

"Inside the pocket of the giant's burlap trousers."

Sebille's face fell.

"The last red feather SB dropped," Hobs exclaimed gleefully.

Sebille gave him rock knuckles, and the two of them turned a united grin and a smug attitude in my direction.

I hesitated for effect, giving them a moment to enjoy their perceived victory. Then I opened my mouth to destroy their happiness. "Third shelf on the fifth shelving unit, center section. Next to the stack of Doctor Osvald's books." I squinted thoughtfully. "The book on top is entitled, *Six Magickal uses for Overripe Bananas and Avocados*."

The duo deflated like last winter's badly tied balloons.

"You're a derf," my lovely assistant informed me.

The front door to the bookstore opened. Lea came inside, frowning. "Hex's collar is miss..."

I pointed to the top of the nearest shelving unit. "It's up there."

"...ing," she finished, her frown deepening. "You know that's getting creepy, right?"

I laughed happily. I was enjoying my newfound skills too much to let them ruin it for me.

My phone rang and I answered with a chirpy, "Croakies Bookstore, Where Magic Happens."

Sebille rolled her eyes and Lea chuckled.

"Is this Naida Griffith, Keeper of the Artifacts?" a gruff voice asked.

My chirpy happiness drained away. "Yes, this is Keeper Naida. Do you need help with an artifact?"

"I do. And it's an emergency."

I grabbed the Book of Pages, intending to call up his problem as he explained it to me. "What's happening?"

"Bessy's disappeared."

I nodded. "Okay, is Bessy your wife? Daughter? Girlfriend?"

"What are you, some kind of sicko?"

I blinked. "Um, no. I'm just trying to get some basic information so I know what I'm up against..."

"Bessy's my best producer. But she's more than that..." The man's voice turned wistful. He sounded like he was near tears. "She's kind of a friend, I guess."

"Can you describe her to me?" I asked, oozing efficiency. I wondered if Grym would be on the case. A missing person would be right up his alley.

The thought depressed me a little. We hadn't been speaking much lately. We'd had a...well... disagreement seemed too mild a term for it.

"Bessy's a hefty girl, with golden hair and soulful brown eyes."

I really should be writing everything down. "Does Bessy have any distinguishing characteristics?"

"Yeah, she's missing," the man on the other end of the line growled.

I bit back a growl of my own. "Can you describe what she was wearing when you last saw her? Clothing, jewelry?"

"Well, Bessy didn't wear too much clothes. But she had a giant brass bell around her neck."

Of course she did.

"So let me recap. I'm looking for a large, naked female with golden hair and soulful brown eyes, wearing a bell."

Sebille, Hobs, and Lea cackled and I had to shush them.

"Look, lady. I ain't never heard of no cows wearin' clothes, but if you think the lack of them clothes makes her naked, then fine. She's naked. Now, can you come out to the farm and look for her. I'm really startin' ta get worried."

I felt all the blood leave my face. "Farm?" My voice squeaked over the word. "You live on a farm?"

His silence was like a thousand Sebille eye rolls. "You didn't think I'd keep a cow in the city, did you?"

"Oh. Yeah. A cow." Did cows bite? Maybe I should bring SB and the sword with me.

I could almost hear the man frown. "You sure you're up to this? I'm startin' ta worry you ain't all there."

I sighed. "No. I'm good. If you'll just give me your address."

"Take the main road West outa town. Turn left at that big tree with the flaking bark and drive about three miles up the gravel road. We're the farm on the left with the giant cow statue in front. You can't miss it."

Yeah, I was pretty sure I could. I thanked him and told him I'd be there as soon as I could, disconnecting as thunder rattled the windows. Rain beat against the glass, wind driving it so hard it sounded like hail.

"We get to go to a farm," I said with forced cheerfulness as I slid my phone into my pocket. Unfortunately, when I looked up, I discovered I was alone in the store.

The derks had run away at the first mention of vast, messy plots of land dotted with large and stinky domestic animals.

Maybe I shouldn't have been so smug about the feather thing.

There's really nothing magical about cow manure. Even when it's mixed into ankle-deep mud, forming an aroma that cannot be described without an entire volume of creative swears.

I tugged against the sucking pull of the muck,

feeling my rubber boot slide away from my foot as I tried to lever it free.

I stopped, jamming my foot back down inside the boot.

"Ribbit!"

The only thing worse than traversing a muddy field in a driving rain was traversing a muddy field in a driving rain with a mouthy frog in my pocket.

"I'm well aware that there's a pond over there, Slimy. You're not going anywhere near it."

"Ribbit?"

I sighed. "Because I don't want to lose you. My luck, you'd jump into it and swim away, and I'd never find you among the lily pads and cattails."

"Meow!"

Miserable in the rain, Wicked shivered beside me, his usually tidy feet coated in slimy muck up to the ankles. I'd tried to carry him across the field, but he was having none of it.

I cast my hopeful gaze toward the small, white farmhouse in the distance. "Maybe you should just run ahead, Mr. Wicked. I'll get there as soon as I can."

Expecting my stalwart cat to refuse to leave me, I watched, shocked and mortally wounded as he took off with a yowl, leaving me in his proverbial dust.

Or muck.

"I see where your loyalties are, you little traitor!" I called after him.

Lightning flashed in the distance. A few seconds later, thunder boomed, seeming to shake the entire world by the roots.

"Ribbit!"

"I'm trying!" I yelled at the frog. I immediately regretted being so cross with the fat little amphibian. It wasn't his fault he was stuck in the middle of a muddy field with me.

I sighed. "Sorry, Slimy. I really wish your driver was on board, though. Maybe Rustin could figure out a way for us to get where we're going."

I missed Rustin for a lot of reasons. Since he'd gone, Slimy hadn't spoken a single word. Though I'd gotten really good at understanding his frog language. I'd thought the two of them had developed separate consciousnesses. The fact that Slimy seemed irreparably changed by Rustin's desertion bothered me. A lot.

I only hoped Rustin was faring better than the frog.

Another world-shaking boom forced me to a decision I knew I was going to regret. I slipped my feet out of the boots and took off running toward the house in my stocking feet.

Well, not running exactly. More like slogging faster without the boots to drag me down.

Mud squished through my toes and splashed up my leg. I grimaced at the slimy feel of it and prayed the sewer-like stench didn't soak into my skin. The last thing I needed was to end up smelling like a dumpster.

The rain turned torrential, pounding onto my soggy head like typewriter keys hitting paper. Lightning arced from the leaden sky, slamming into a tree a mere fifteen feet away. I screamed, my foot glancing off the edge of a water-filled cow bump, which Farmer Blue had warned me about. They were deep holes caused by cows slogging through a muddy pasture. I fell over, my entire left side splashing into icy water.

That was the last straw. I had to change course.

I wasn't going to make it to the farmhouse.

I climbed to my feet and switched directions, heading toward the old barn in the near distance.

I hit the enormous sliding door at a run, palms slapping into the moist wood as I pressed closer in the hopes the ancient structure would protect me just by its nearness and sheer size. I shoved the door open just enough to squeeze through, and stood shivering in the silty dirt. It was drier inside the old wooden building than I'd assumed it would be. Quieter.

Lightning struck again and I jumped, squealing. The strike had sounded terrifyingly close.

Leaving the sliding door open a couple of feet to allow the dove-gray light of the overcast day inside, I moved farther into the space, looking around.

The floor of the barn was dirt mixed with hay

and wood shavings. The place smelled like fresh hay, the air sweet and surprisingly clean.

I hadn't expected that.

The other thing I hadn't expected were the inquisitive gazes of the cows. Gathered together in a large enclosure on one end, with an open door to the field beyond, my bovine barn-mates chewed thoughtfully as they eyed my disheveled self. Their ears twitched flies away as they chewed, the tags showing white in the dim light.

I knew from my quick conversation with Farmer Blue that he kept dairy cows. I looked around for the equipment he used to milk them and saw nothing but a few pitchforks and a couple of metal bins along the sidewall that I assumed contained grain.

The loft that was above their heads was filled with stacked green cubes of hay, and a wooden ladder attached to the loft seemed the only way to access the higher spot.

I looked longingly up at that fresh, clean hay and sighed. I was not a farm girl by any stretch of the imagination. But I'd always had a thing for haylofts and green, sweet-smelling hay.

I was oh-so-tempted to climb that ladder and take a nap in the soft hay. The strenuous activity had worn me out.

I shook my head. No, I'd wait by the door until the storm died down and then head for the house.

Yawning widely, I decided I needed a cup of Sebille's energy tea.

The plan to wait by the door lasted all of five minutes. The steel-gray clouds high above just kept coming. As one angry-looking bank of the things moved on past, it was replaced by another, even angrier looking bank.

I was clearly going to be in that barn for a while.

Shivering violently, I turned and looked longingly up at the loft, making a sudden decision. It would be warmer up there. Maybe there'd be an old horse blanket or something I could wrap myself up in. I'd just take a few minutes to rest my eyes and dry off.

Decision made, I looked down at Mr. Slimy, who'd been suspiciously quiet since our sprint to the barn. "You'll like the loft," I assured him happily. "I'm sure there will be lots of spiders and stuff for you to eat up there."

He fixed his blank, black gaze on me and puffed his throat unhelpfully.

Slipping him into the pocket of my jacket, I headed for the wooden ladder. I was eager to check out the loft and happy I'd found an excuse to do it.

A chilly breeze wafted through the door and hay sifted down onto my head.

A muffled thumping rose above the cow enclosure. I peered down on them as I started climbing up the ladder, finding them still chewing and staring, their bovine heads lifting to follow my progress upward.

"Nothing to see here, girls," I told them. "These are not the drones you're looking for."

A clump of hay hit me in the face, some of it falling into my open mouth. "Ugh!" I spit it out, plucking at my tongue to remove some pieces that stuck there.

"Whathh in the worldth?"

The ladder wobbled, and I looked up in surprise. Footsteps pounded over the rungs. Another clump of hay sifted past me.

I sneezed, my eyes closing for just a beat and when I reopened them I saw a face, just a flash of eyes with a greasy fringe of hair falling over a grungy face, and then something shoved my shoulders, and I was suddenly sailing backward, toward the hard, dusty ground below.

2

SPINNING COW UDDERS! WILL YOU
PLEASE STOP THAT?

*a*t the last moment, I remembered to twist my body to protect Slimy in my pocket. I hit the ground hard, the impact knocking the air from my lungs and doubling me over as I struggled to breathe.

A panicked croaking sounded from inside my pocket. As soon as I could drag air into my lungs, I reached inside to grab the frog and make sure he was okay.

He promptly peed on my hand.

I didn't even have enough air in my lungs to complain.

The ladder juddered and I remembered someone had been on it with me. Someone I couldn't see. I hated invisible stuff. Nothing good ever came from invisible stuff. I put Slimy in my lap and shoved against the floor, crab walking backward with my gaze locked on the ladder.

The barn quaked under another violent boom beyond the ancient wood walls, and a fresh deluge noisily thrummed against the metal roof.

Wheezing and gasping for air, I shoved to my feet and backed away from the ladder. It didn't move for a long moment and I started to think whatever it was had left.

Then I heard a bell tinkling.

I frowned.

Beyond the big doors, lightning speared the sky and thunder followed right on its heels.

The ladder juddered again.

Ribbit!

Slimy's bulging black eyes peered toward the ladder, unblinking. His throat worked steadily and he gave off the general air of someone who didn't like what he was seeing.

I really wished he'd talk to me.

"What is it, Slimy? Do you see something?"

Ribbit.

"Yeah, unless someone has a Frog-to-English dictionary, that's not going to do me much good."

Without warning, Slimy leaped from my lap.

I gave a startled scream as he hit a pile of dusty hay and jumped again, heading directly for the ladder. "Slimy, no!"

He, of course, ignored me and kept hopping. I ran to try to catch him, my hands clasping empty air multiple times before he stopped, his tongue snapping out to tug a spider out of an enormous web between the rungs of the ladder.

I sighed. "This is no time for you to decide to eat, Slimy. We have an invisible…"

Slam!

I screamed, pressing my palm against my pounding chest as I looked toward the enclosure holding the cattle.

Slam!

One of the cows, a large black one, was kicking the wall of the enclosure, her brown eyes staring in my direction.

My pulse was somewhere around my ears, my heart pounding against my ribs. Between the thunder booming outside and the cows trying to send me to the stars inside, I was seriously on edge. "What?" I demanded of the cow.

Slam!

My nerve endings rose up out of my skin and did a panicked little jig, preparing to send me into full-on hysteria. "What do you want? Why can't anybody talk to me?"

Slam!

I jumped again, giving an angry little scream.

Thinking there might be something inside the enclosure the cow was afraid of, I looked over the wall of the cow pen, seeing nothing but dirt, hay and enormous cow patties, a.k.a. poops, on the floor. Maybe there was a mouse or some...

Slam!

"Erghhh! *Spinning cow udders*! Will you please stop that?"

The cow turned its head at my outburst and stared at me a minute, then walked away from the wall and shoved its way into the crowd around the hay feeder.

I sagged against the wall.

Tinkle, tinkle.

Hot breath bathed my neck. I screamed, jumped sideways and did the high step toward the middle of the barn.

I watched in horror as the dirt puffed up along the floor, heading right for me.

Tinkle, tinkle.

Hot breath wafted past, followed by a snuffling sound and then something large and wet slipped over my face.

It felt like a...tongue?

Then it hit me. "Bessy?"

Snorfle, snorfle, lick.

I ran my sleeve over my wet cheek. "Well, you certainly are a friendly invisible cow, aren't you?"

Tinkle, tinkle.

The bell was going to come in handy. It should be easy to find her with the bell tinkling helpfully.

Reluctantly, due to my awareness of the tooth-filled mouth nearby and the enormous size of the creature, I reached a tentative hand in Bessy's direction. I felt velvety smooth skin with large, moist holes in it. I sank knuckle-deep in a nostril. "*Singing chicken gizzards!*" Yanking my hand back, I dragged it over my wet and muddy jeans, adding to the frog pee I'd already wiped there.

I lowered my hand and reached again, hoping to grab the bell around Bessy's neck. I could hold her there and give Farmer Blue a call. My job had been to find the cow. I'd done that. I was thinking maybe that would be good enough. Even as I had the thought, I knew I couldn't leave it at that. There was clearly a magical artifact at work and it was my job to find it.

Sometimes I hated my job.

My fingers closed over something cool and metallic. The bell. "Gotcha!" I said softly.

Boom!

Thunder shook the barn again. Bessy jerked away from my grip, and the rope holding the bell came loose in my hand. I looked down as the faint shape of a brass cowbell formed in my palm and then thickened, becoming visible. The rope that hung from the bell was worn through as if Bessy had been rubbing it against something for a while.

I looked up from the bell, squinting. "Bessy? Are you still there?" Maybe the fact that I could see the bell meant that whatever had been keeping her out of sight was failing.

Could I be that lucky?

Boom!

Slam!

Tinkle, tinkle.

Not a chance. The tinkling of the bell no longer pointed to where Bessy was. And walking forward, gently waving my arms, I didn't feel her nearby.

I sighed. Bessy was gone. I would need to make my way to the farmhouse and give Farmer Blue the bad news. But first I needed to gather up my frog. I glanced toward the ladder. "Slimy?" Where was the little guy? "Slimy, come on, we need to go talk to the client."

I listened for a soft *ribbit* beneath the pounding of the rain on the roof and walls.

Silence.

"Slimy?" Dropping to my knees beside the ladder, I ran my hands through the loose, dusty hay that littered nearly every inch of the barn floor, looking around, under and behind the wooden ladder.

No Slimy.

A sense of dread filled my chest. My stomach twisted with fear.

Had Slimy been lost to the same artifact as Bessy?

"Please, no!" I muttered as panic turned my insides to mush.

Slam!

A steaming cup of tea appeared in front of my face. I shivered violently, pulling the hand-knitted blanket closer around my shoulders and looked up into the pink-cheeked round face of Mrs. Farmer Blue. "Thank you."

She patted my shoulder with a chubby hand. "You're welcome, dear. Don't worry. Your little pet will show up."

I sipped my tea, keeping my face averted so she couldn't see the doubt in my expression. I'd looked everywhere for Slimy, spent an hour turning the barn over in an attempt to find him. It was as if he'd simply disappeared.

Poof.

Farmer Blue sat across from me at the table, staring down at the dusty cowbell I'd brought back with me. He hadn't said five words since I'd returned with the bad news that I'd had his favorite cow in my hands and had lost her again. "I'm really sorry about Bessy," I told him.

He made a harrumphing type sound and continued to stare at the bell.

Meow!

I looked down into Wicked's judgmental orange gaze. He blamed me for losing Slimy. Or maybe he was mad because I'd lost Bessy the cow. I couldn't be sure of anything except that he was mad. Holding my gaze, he very deliberately rubbed himself across Mrs. Blue's stout shins.

"What a pretty boy you are," Mrs. Blue crooned, bending to scratch Mr. Wicked behind his traitorous ears. "And so sweet he is too."

"Yeah," I grumbled crankily. "Sweet."

Wicked purred loudly in defiance, trotting back over to the small dish that had recently held canned tuna fish mixed with fresh cream. If I didn't get him out of the Blue kitchen fast, he was going to gain five pounds and leave me behind like yesterday's stinky trash.

"You want some more, sweet boy?" Mrs. Farmer Blue hurried over and picked up the dish as Mr. Wicked twined eagerly around her ankles, nearly tripping the poor woman as she tried to scoop tuna into the dish.

"What kind of magic is this?" Farmer Blue asked, his brows lowered over question-filled hazel eyes.

I wish I knew. But I couldn't tell him that. "Have you recently purchased any new equipment for the barn?"

He shook his head. "Nah. Everything I have was passed down from my Da and his. There's nothin' newer than me in that old barn."

I couldn't help thinking that the same could be said of the house, judging by the small rounded refrigerator, the massive stove that I was pretty sure was fueled by wood, and the ancient cabinets that looked as if they had an inch of paint on them.

Mrs. Blue settled the dish back in front of my disloyal cat and he dove in, tail whipping happily behind him and his purr coating the air like the layers of paint covered the cabinets.

"Any new animals?" I asked.

He thought about that for a beat and shook his head.

"There's an opossum that's moved into the hayloft," Mrs. Blue said, wiping her hands on the old-fashioned apron she wore over her flower-print cotton dress.

"That opossum ain't disappearin' my cows," Farmer Blue groused. "This here's some kind of ugly magic."

His wife rolled her eyes. "There's no such thing as magic Foster." She looked at me, giving me a smile. "Isn't that right, young lady?"

I blinked and looked at Farmer Blue. He shrugged. "She refuses to believe. But I had a cousin who was light in the loafers. I know there's things in the world that defy explanation."

I sat there a moment, wondering how to address the questions suddenly flooding my mind. Finally, I settled for the obvious. "Light in the loafers?"

He got a disgusted look on his ruddy face. "You know, a fairy."

I opened my mouth and then closed it. Opened it again and made a slightly alarmed sound. Surely he wasn't calling a gay man a fairy?

Surely.

The air before me sparkled and I realized my mistake as the tiny form of Shirley the cranky Pixie started to form on the air. "Oh! Sorry. I *but*? dialed you by mistake (spelling intentional), Shirley. You can go away!"

A tiny, irritated face appeared in a burst of magical sparks, and the Pixie huffed with frustration before she ground out, "Don't call me!" and disappeared in a flash of white light.

As the supernormal world's Witch-a-pedia, Shirley the Pixie was the reluctant source of tons of valuable magical information she'd much rather not share. She hated being summoned. She probably hated it even more when she was summarily dismissed after an accidental summoning.

"What was that with all the sparkles," Farmer Blue asked, frowning as he poked a calloused digit into the air where Shirley had been.

I glanced at Mrs. Farmer Blue. She'd turned away and was busying herself washing things in the sink. Something about her brisk, slightly jerky movements told me she'd seen the Pixie's almost-arrival.

I decided denial was the best course of action. "Huh? What?"

Farmer Blue's face folded into a perplexed scowl.

"Tell me more about this cousin you mentioned," I urged.

Blue grunted. "Percival. He had a strange way about him. And he was always popping away and then popping back again." Blue shook his head. "I saw him disappear into thin air once."

I relaxed, realizing the curmudgeonly farmer *had* meant an actual magical Fairy. "By any chance, has Percival been here lately?"

"Nah. He disappeared a while ago and never came back."

I stared at him, my brows skimming my hairline.

After a moment, he seemed to understand why I was looking at him with a giant unibrow. "Ah, hah. Not like that. He didn't disappear like Bessy." He chuckled softly. "He climbed into his tiny pink car and headed for a rainbow screaming something about dancing a jig at the end. I don't know if he ever found the end of that rainbow. But I always said I wished him well."

My brows stuck to my dark brown hair for a moment longer and then fell back where they belonged. I had no idea what the man was talking about. But I refused to dig any deeper into it for fear I'd get caught in the hallucinogenic-like visions living in his mind and never find my way out again.

I was starting to understand why Mrs. Farmer Blue pretended she didn't believe in magic. It was probably just easier that way.

I stood, reluctantly shrugging the blanket off my still-damp shoulders. I needed to get home and get into some dry clothes. And I needed to hit the books, looking for a magical artifact that made things invisible. Maybe it was some kind of farm implement or a spelled farm animal.

Once I had an idea what I was dealing with, I'd come back with help if I had to drag Sebille and Lea there kicking and screaming.

Slimy's life...and Bessy's too...were at stake. I wouldn't be taking no for an answer.

3

BEWARE QUILLERANS BEARING SMALL BASKETS

"*N*o," Sebille said, glowering at me across the sales counter in the bookstore.

"You *have* to come with me," I said in a voice that sounded desperate and whiny even to me. "I lost Slimy!"

That did seem to make a dent in her steely resistance. "I'm sure he's fine," she said. But I could tell she wasn't fully convinced.

"Lea's coming," I told the defiant Sprite, a.k.a. my assistant. "She's making up a spell to illuminate invisible things."

My information didn't work out quite the way I'd hoped.

"Good. Then you don't need me." Sebille slammed the spell book she'd been perusing closed with a bang and spun on her shiny red heel, stalking toward the back room. I glanced down at the book, reading the title with interest. *How to Magically remove Freckles, Birthmarks, and Age Spots.*

Hmm, since Sebille had no birthmarks and she wasn't nearly old enough for age spots, I realized she was researching how to get rid of her freckles. Interesting. I'd never known the spots that covered her long, lean face bothered her. I just accepted them as something that came with her fire-red hair and pale skin.

Shaking off the thought, I huffed out a frustrated breath as the door slammed shut between the two sections of the collective space called Croakies. My business was comprised of a magical bookstore in the front and a library of magical artifacts in the back. As the Librarian in charge of magical artifacts, it was my job to find and wrangle missing and out-of-control artifacts and bring them back to Croakies to be filed safely away.

Unfortunately for me, in the current instance, I needed Sebille's help. I could admit to myself that I was woefully inadequate to most artifact wrangling tasks all alone. But I'd never tell the Sprite I needed her. That way lay much future emotional pain. And pretty much world-ending, apocalyptic-level ego explosions.

The bell on the door jangled. I turned to find my second favorite witch coming through the door. Lea was, of course, my first favorite witch. Even if she *had* left me to make my way alone among the cow patties. Grumble.

Maude Quilleran had a wide smile on her face and a small basket in her hand. My faithless cat, who still wasn't speaking to me since we'd left the Blue's farm without his best bud, Slimy, ran to greet Maude with a happy yowl and a window-rattling purr.

Maude crouched down to greet him with a wide grin. "Hello there, handsome." She set the tiny basket onto the carpet and scooped up my cat, hugging him against her chest and kissing him between his perky gray ears. "It's so nice to see you again."

The teen witch had been responsible for giving me Wicked. Once upon a time, I'd done her a small favor involving a magical hairbrush, and she'd wanted to repay me. I'd resisted, knowing that the fifteen minutes of my time wasn't worth enough to take the teenager's hard-earned allowance from her. So she'd surprised me with a tiny gray kitten. I'd later learned the gift was a much bigger one than I'd known. And Maude had given him to me at great personal risk. For those reasons and more, I would forever be grateful to her for bringing Wicked into my life.

Even when he was acting like a frog's butt about a...erm...frog's butt.

I gave the young girl a hug, smashing Wicked between us until he yowled with displeasure. "How are you? I haven't seen you in weeks."

Maude settled Mr. Wicked to his feet and retrieved the basket. "I know. I'm sorry. We've been busy working with Rustin."

Rustin was Maude's cousin and the victim of the Quilleran family's darker inclinations. He'd been spelled into Mr. Slimy when I first met him, destined to fade away into frogginess if I didn't work against a literal clock to save him.

Unfortunately, we hadn't been able to totally extract him from the frog...at least not until recently...but the work of his Aunt Madeline Quilleran and Maude had saved his soul from being sucked into the frog's essence, and had given Slimy magical intelligence he shouldn't have had as a frog.

"How is Rustin? I kind of miss the annoying guy."

Maude giggled. "That's why I'm here, partly." She held up the basket. "This is the other reason. I wondered if you might be willing to help Sadie."

"Sadie?" I eyed the basket as a wave of trepidation swept over me. *Beware Quillerans bearing small baskets*, my mind screamed at me. "Who's Sadie?"

"Not who," Maude said, flipping the lid back on the basket and reaching inside. "What."

I blinked, my eyes going wide. Maude had

grabbed a tiny piece of rainbow from the basket and was holding it in one hand, her pretty face filled with hope. "This is Sadie. She's very sweet. I'm sure Mr. Slimy will like her."

I narrowed my gaze on the little witch. "You brought me a lizard?"

Maude flushed. "She's not a lizard exactly."

Something in the way she said it warned me I should pay close attention to the "not exactly" part of her response. "What exactly is she?"

Maude chewed her bottom lip.

The brightly hued reptile in her hand blinked slowly, lifting her tiny head as if trying to figure out what I was. I narrowed my eyes at the little creature, returning the favor. She did remind me of someone, though I couldn't quite pinpoint who.

"Well, technically, I guess she is a lizard. A reptile anyway."

My gaze jerked to Maude and she flushed guiltily. "How is it that you brought me a creature which you've apparently named already, and you have no idea what she is?"

Maude expelled her breath in a huff. "She's a rare amalgamate dragon from the rainforests of Hawaii."

A lot of questions flitted through my mind, but I went with the first and easiest. "Why?"

"Sadie was involved in our experiments with

Rustin. But she's not a good fit for what we're trying to do. Aunt Maddie was going to...dispose of her." Maude's lips thinned and tightened with disgust. "I just couldn't let that happen."

I felt my eyes go wide. "Dispose of her?"

The little creature in Maude's hand warbled softly, her slanted eyes turning turquoise for a moment and then going black again. Whatever she was, she was adorable. I couldn't let her be... disposed of...could I?

The door between the store and the library flew open and crashed against the wall. I jumped and whipped around, glaring at the Sprite.

She didn't even notice.

Sebille's gaze locked onto Maude's hand, and she strode forward faster than I'd ever seen her move unless she was being threatened...or heading for a plate of egg rolls. She stopped in front of the young witch, her pale, freckled face filled with awe, and wordlessly extended her hands.

Maude carefully placed the creature across Sebille's outstretched palms.

Sadie warbled again. Her eyes glowed with pretty aqua light, and the light sifted along her body, fading to white as it slid off the tip of her tail.

"Amazing," Sebille whispered.

Maude and I shared a look.

"Do you know what she is?" I asked.

Sebille nodded. "Yes. She's incredible." Sebille turned and headed back toward the library, her gaze never leaving the creature on her palms. Sadie stared back, seemingly just as transfixed by Sebille as the Sprite was by her.

"Thanks for bringing her to me," Sebille said at the door. Then she disappeared into the artifact library without another word.

As the door snicked shut, Maude and I shared a look.

"Crab's crutches." I shook my head. "I guess Sadie's staying. What did you want to tell me about Rustin?"

"He wanted me to let you know that he's all right."

I nodded, filled with relief. I hadn't spoken to him in weeks, and I'd been starting to worry that his work with his aunt wasn't going well. "Any progress in helping him find a body?"

"Some. At least we have a general direction now. A plan." She frowned. "There have been some hiccups."

I could imagine. "What kind of hiccups?"

She shook her head. "Aunt Maddie told me I couldn't talk about it."

I held my thumb and forefinger half an inch apart. "Just a little?" I wheedled.

She grimaced. "We've given up on Rustin finding a permanent body."

My smile slid away, and my stomach twisted with despair. "Oh no."

Maude saw my reaction and shook her head, reaching out to touch my arm. "No, it's not bad news. Not really. We've come up with a good compromise. Rustin's fully on board with it." Despite her upbeat reporting, I could see the doubt and worry in her yellow eyes.

"What's the compromise?"

"I really shouldn't..."

"Please," I asked, my heart in the single, desperate plea. "He's my friend. I feel responsible for his predicament. Tell me?"

"Well, first of all, you are *not* responsible, Naida."

I shrugged, feeling the old guilt flooding back at the news that their experiments had failed.

"We're going to twist Rustin's essence to give him dual physicality."

She looked so proud I felt stupid having to ask the eighteen-year-old what she meant. "Huh?"

"Like a shape-shifter. We got the idea from Margot."

Margot Quilleran was one of the black witches in the Quilleran coven. She was evil and deadly, her ginormous owl form the most terrifying monster I'd ever encountered. I felt my eyes go wide. "Margot's helping?"

"No. Are you kidding? She mostly paces her cage all day, spitting nails at us through her eyes. But she has shifter DNA, and we're using it to help Rustin find a form he can shift into."

I was starting to warm to the idea. Then I realized what she was saying. "Wait. He'll have to be some kind of animal? How is that better than being stuck inside Slimy?"

"He'll have a dual nature, Naida. He'll be both."

"He can be himself?"

"Part of the time. We're not sure yet how much time he'll need to spend in his second form. But we do know that, with time, he can extend the time for each or both."

"That's wonderful!" For the first time in weeks, I felt hope for Rustin.

Maude bounced happily on her toes. "I know, right?"

On an impulse, I hugged her. "Thanks for coming to tell me. Do you want to stay for tea? I'm pretty sure I have some cookies left if Hobs didn't find them."

My resident Hobgoblin was death to sweets of any kind. Especially if they had chocolate in them. I'd baked a batch of chocolate chips the night before and hidden them all around Croakies. If they were spread out all over the place, I figured it would at least take him longer to find them all.

"I'd love some!"

As I fixed tea, Maude looked around the shop. Wicked was sitting in a beam of sun on the windowsill, licking his paws. Maude walked over and peered down into Mr. Slimy's terrarium. "Where is he? Is he hiding under his rock?" The young witch reached into the glass box and lifted the flat-topped rock I'd situated under a heating lamp.

"Not exactly." I handed her a cup of tea and, glancing around first to make sure Hobs was nowhere to be seen, I walked over to the first set of shelves and extracted a thick cookbook, reaching behind it to retrieve a small plastic container of cookies.

I settled the container on the round reading table and sat down with Maude after grabbing my own cup of tea.

I let her enjoy her snack for a minute before I gave her the bad news. "Slimy's disappeared."

Maude stopped chewing, her eyes going wide. "He what?"

I quickly filled her in on my Farmer Blue problem. She listened carefully and then finished her cookie with a thoughtful expression on her face.

"Have you heard of anything like that before," I asked the young witch.

She surprised me by nodding. "It wasn't a spell, though. I'm not even sure it was an artifact." Her gaze when it lifted to mine was worried. "It sounds to me like a split in the dimensional fabric."

Well, that sounded bad. And I was pretty sure I couldn't just buy dimension-repairing thread and needle and sew it back up. "How do we fix that?" I asked Maude.

"I have no idea. But Aunt Maddie might. You'd better come back to the house with me."

Well, blithering bat boogers.

4

AND NOT A MOMENT MORE!

"*I*t can't be this easy," I lamented in a voice that was more than a little bit whiny.

Maude laughed as she shoved the car door closed. She looked up and waved at the long line of red-eyed vultures sitting atop her aunt's castle-like home. "I don't know what to tell you, Naida."

"It took you like ten minutes to get here. Normally it takes me hours. And there were no narrow, winding roads with plunging cliffs on both sides. No deadly forests. No switchbacks, turn-arounds, or stomach twisting hills. You took like three turns and we were here."

"The Universe is protective of PTB, you know that."

And Maude's aunt was one of them. The Powers That Be were like the politicians of the magical

Universe. They were its eyes and ears in each dimension.

I *did* know that, which was why I was surprised the Universe had let Maude just drive right up to the house. *In ten frog flipping minutes!*

The teen looked at my face and giggled. "I live here, Naida."

The line of vultures lifted their wings in that wave thing they did, the movement sifting along the roofline like they were fans at a witchy baseball game. I didn't know if the wave was a warning, a magical key to open the door, or just a "Hey, how are ya?" to guests.

I kind of doubted it was that last thing, though.

The front door opened as Maude and I approached. I tensed, expecting Madeline to appear from the darkness on the other side like she had the last two times, her angular face looking like something out of a scary scene from a Grimm's Fairy Tale.

The space on the other side of the door was empty. There was nobody there. As soon as I cleared the door, Maude flicked a finger and it closed behind us. "Auntie, I'm home!"

I nearly laughed. I'd spent so many hours in complete and utter terror of the uber-powerful Madeline Quilleran, that I had trouble envisioning her as *Auntie, I'm home* material.

"In the kitchen," a familiar voice said, the tone

lighter than I usually heard from Madeline Quilleran.

Maude jerked her head toward the hallway leading to the kitchen.

I started after her, feeling the glossy brown gaze of the stag over the fireplace following my movements. My shoulder blades prickled at the feeling. But I could never catch the thing in the act of spying on me.

I jerked to a stop, my head whipping around, hoping to catch the dead deer head watching me. The eyes were blank, focused toward the center of the big room. Not on me. I narrowed my gaze on it for a moment and then headed toward the kitchen, hearing the soft chuff of something on the air behind me. The stag was laughing.

Dang magical wall deco.

Maude was sitting at the long granite table, a cup of tea steaming on the glossy surface before her. She was taking a bite from a biscuit when I entered the room and her eyes rose to mine, a question filling her gaze.

I felt compelled to explain. "I got lost."

She chuckled. "You were trying to catch Felonius again, weren't you?"

"Felonius?"

"The stag," a deeper, more mature female voice said.

I turned to look at Madeline, finding her

standing before the sink with a steaming cup in her hand. She gave me a slightly scary smile. "He *is* watching you. But you won't catch him at it. He's much too quick and smart for that."

"We'll just see about that," I murmured under my breath.

"Yes," Madeline said, her expression pleasant enough to melt butter. "We will."

My cheeks heated. I hadn't intended for her to hear me. "Did Maude tell you why I'm here?"

Madeline moved toward me, her steps so graceful and light she appeared to be floating above the tiles. The floor-length dress she wore didn't do anything to remove that perception. I watched her carefully, my pulse spiking as she drew quickly near. "Sit," she instructed, placing the tea on the table next to where Maude sat. "Would you like a sweet biscuit?"

I swallowed, my throat and mouth suddenly dry, and nodded. "Please." I really didn't want the biscuit. But it would give me something to do with my hands when I got really nervous. So I didn't make a complete fool of myself.

I choked on the first bite of the biscuit, my coughing fit nearly making me gag.

So much for not making a fool of myself.

"I understand you've found a dimensional wrinkle."

I frowned. "I'm not sure. Maude said that's what

it sounded like. I was leaning toward a rogue artifact."

She lifted a dark brow. "Have you found an artifact?"

"Well, no, but..."

Madeline nodded as if she'd proven her point. "I've heard of this one other time, a hundred years ago. That wrinkle grew until it consumed an entire town." She frowned. "Messy business."

I really didn't like the sound of that. "When you say consumed, what do you mean, exactly?"

Madeline shrugged, clearly not interested in the fate of that unlucky town. "Gone. Kaput."

"Did they ever come back?"

"Not that I know of. We managed to stop the wrinkle from growing, but, unfortunately, it necessitated cutting the wrinkle at its base and removing it." She sighed. "Doing dimensional surgery is such tedious work. I'll have to cancel my appointments for the week."

"Wait a minute!" I shoved the deadly biscuit away and rested my arms on the table, leaning closer to Madeline as if the smaller distance would make her words less terrifying. "You can't just slice this thing off. Slimy's in there." And Bessy, I needed to keep reminding myself.

Madeline's yellow gaze widened. "The frog? What in the world is he doing there?"

I wished I knew. "He came with me to the barn. We were looking for Bessy the cow…"

Madeline held up a slender hand. "You brought the frog to a client site?"

"Yes, I…"

"Why?" Her question didn't appear to be a frivolous one. She seemed genuinely interested in a clinical sense.

I tensed, not wanting Madeline to get too interested in Slimy. Having a witch interested in any of your friends was dangerous. And Slimy had already been through enough magical malfeasance for one small, green life.

For all I knew, that could be the reason for his froggy incontinence issues.

I'm just sayin'.

"I don't know. Wicked came along and he wanted me to bring Slimy."

Rather than put Madeline off Slimy's scent, my explanation seemed to make her even more interested. "The Familiar is bonded to the frog?"

I couldn't help noticing that she'd said "The" instead of "Your" Familiar. I tried not to take it personally. I mean, I wasn't a witch, I was a sorceress. We generally didn't have Familiars. "No…I mean… they like each other," I stuttered lamely.

Finally, Maude saved me. "The cat formed a bond when Rustin was in residence," the young witch said with careful nonchalance. "He probably doesn't realize Rustin's gone."

Madeline seemed to lose interest in the subject. "Well, that doesn't matter now. We have to close the wrinkle, Naida. If we don't it will grow and keep consuming more and more land. It could conceivably suck the entirety of Enchanted into another dimension."

"How much time do I have?"

"For what?"

"To get Slimy back?"

"It's not possible to get someone back, Sorceress. Have you not been listening to me?"

I stood up. "How long?"

Madeline sighed. "It will take me two days to prepare the spell. Once I begin, nothing can interfere. Any disturbance of the spell at that point would cause a cataclysmic explosion and create a massive black hole. Enchanted and a good part of the surrounding countryside would get sucked into the abyss and lost forever."

"So you wouldn't be open to say...stretching it to three days?"

"Naida, keeper!" Madeline said, her voice booming around the kitchen and rattling the glass in the pretty picture windows.

I raised my hands in surrender. "Okay, okay. I've got it. Forty-eight hours." I turned on my heel and headed toward the front door. "Give or take a few hours," I murmured so softly I barely heard it myself.

"Forty-eight hours and not a moment more!" Madeline boomed.

I stuck my tongue out at the stag as I hurried past. Childish, yes. But it made me feel better. I was standing on the porch, my gaze drawn to the giant, hostile birds circling above my head before I remembered I needed Maude to take me home.

The young witch came outside a few minutes later, grinning when she saw me sitting on the steps waiting. "You didn't want to come back inside and face Aunt Maddie again, did you?" She handed me another sweet biscuit as she walked past.

"I was just enjoying the pleasant temperatures. If the sun could find a way past the thousands of massive, red-eyed guard birds in the sky, it might be really nice out."

Maude giggled, sliding behind the steering wheel. "You're funny, Naida."

I bit into my biscuit, the sweet, buttery taste bathing my taste buds in nirvana. "Your aunt hates me."

Maude backed her little car out of the parking space at breakneck speed, barely even glancing behind to make sure she wasn't going to hit a tree or something. She drove with the reckless abandon of a teenager who believed she was bulletproof and immortal. "Maybe if you didn't tweak her all the time..." She rolled her eyes in my direction, a smile still riding her pretty face.

I shrugged. "I've been hanging around Sebille too long."

We drove in silence for a few moments while I thought about my wrinkle problem. When my head started hurting, I turned to Maude. "Do you know anything about fixing a wrinkle?"

Maude turned off the highway, heading toward downtown and Croakies. "A giant glob of anti-aging cream?"

"Har," I responded, sighing. After what I'd recently experienced with an anti-aging cream that had worked too well...wayyyyy too well...I didn't find that funny.

Much.

"Don't worry, Naida. I have a feeling you're going to be getting some help soon."

"What does that mean?"

She shrugged, a secret little smile on her face. "Here we are."

I fixed a narrowed gaze on her for a long moment. She simply stared back, a tiny dimple decorating her flushed cheek. Shaking my head, I climbed out of the car. "Thanks for taking me to your aunt's place." I leaned down and looked across the car. "If you think of anything that will help..."

"I'll let you know. In the meantime, don't you have a Hobgoblin at the store now?"

"I do, but I don't see how..."

"Bye, Naida." She drove away, nearly jerking the door out of my hand as I hurried to close it before she left.

I stood on the sidewalk watching the little car fly down the street and whip around the corner as if it were being chased by the hounds of Hades.

"Hobs? What had she asked about him?" At a loss, I headed into Croakies and was nearly mown down to the well-worn carpet the moment I stepped through the door.

"Naida!"

I yelped in surprise, my hand going to my chest as Sebille flew toward me. She was holding the rainbow lizard carefully in front of her. "You won't believe..."

"What's wrong? What did Hobs and Wicked do now?"

Sebille shook her head. "They didn't..."

I trudged past her and shoved my purse behind the sales counter. "We have a big problem. Slimy's in danger. We only have two days, and I have no idea how to save him. Or Bessy." I frowned. "How am I going to get inside a dimensional wrinkle, fetch Slimy and the cow, and get back out?" I looked up at Sebille, who was standing in front of me with a grin still on her face.

"Why are you holding that creature? And you're

grinning at me. You know it makes me uncomfortable when you grin at me."

"Hello, Naida."

The voice didn't register at first. I blinked, my mind trying to wrap itself around what I'd heard.

And then it hit me. *Rustin*?

5

AT LAST A FRIEND

*M*y gaze whipped around.

Rustin was standing a few feet away, looking solid and happy and...really good.

Not trusting that he was real, I didn't try to touch him. I couldn't face the disappointment if he was a figment of my imagination. Goddess knew, if Sebille was grinning at me, it was highly possible I was stroking out on the spot. "I..." I forced my mouth to close and swallowed. "Rustin? How?"

Sebille laughed gaily.

I jumped, looking at her as if she'd been replaced by a doppelganger. But that wouldn't be right either. Doppelgangers generally represented the ugly side of a person's personality. The evil side. But then Sebille's normal personality was pretty ugly. So maybe...

Yeah, I was definitely having a stroke. I reached up to see if one side of my face felt funny.

"It's really him, Naida," the Sprite told me. "He's back."

I looked at the witch, my gaze forming a silent question.

He nodded. "It's true. Well, mostly. I'm here for a while. I can't stay."

The hope that had started to build in my soul sizzled and died, leaving me with a crestfallen look. "You can't stay?"

"Probably not..."

Sebille hurried over and held up her hands, showing me the cute, multi-hued dragon, lizard thing. The little creature cocked its adorable head at me and burped, blowing pink and green and purple smoke into the air. "He's hiding in Sadie."

Crestfallen transformed to confused. My poor face was going to have muscle spasms at the current rate of emotional upheaval. "I don't understand."

"The experiments with Margot have been..." his handsome face folded into a frown. "Intense. I just needed some time to rest."

As if his words were a veil being pulled away from him, I noticed the purple arcs beneath his piercing blue gaze and the weary slope of his broad shoulders.

Tired he might be, but he was still adorable.

A few years older than me, Rustin had thick,

black hair that fell over his forehead to give him a boyish look and a classically perfect nose. He wore wire-rimmed spectacles that made him look slightly geeky, which I found irresistible.

Sebille's words finally sunk in. "You're hiding? Madeline doesn't know you're here?"

"Hopefully, she doesn't know I'm even gone. Not yet."

Sebille held Sadie up to her face and touched noses with the little creature, making nauseating cooing noises.

I grimaced, glancing at Rustin and finding him grinning. Suddenly, the reality sank in, and color infused my face as pleasure blossomed. "You're really here."

He opened his arms and I hurried into them, resting my head against a delightfully solid chest. He felt warm and wonderfully real. "You're not ethereal anymore?" I could no longer call him ghost witch. Though the habit was pretty ingrained. I'd probably still do it.

He laughed. "No. During the time I'm able to be outside of my host, I'm perfectly normal."

"What's Madeline going to do when she finds out you're gone," I asked.

"She'll be irritated. As soon as she figures out where I've gone, she'll probably yank me back."

Sebille's bright green eyes went wide. "What about Sadie?"

Rustin shrugged. "I just don't know. Maude assured me she'd be safe."

"This was Maude's spell?" As soon as I said the words, I realized the answer was obvious. Maude had orchestrated the whole thing. "She helped you get away. Madeline's not going to be happy."

"No," he agreed. "But she thinks the sun rises and sets on that girl. Maude will be able to exert some control on Maddie."

"Hopefully, my problem will help. It should keep Madeline busy for a couple of days anyway."

"What problem?" Rustin asked. He dropped gracefully into a chair at the little reading table by the shelves.

"I'll make tea," Sebille said, happily.

I quickly filled him in on the dimensional wrinkle and my worries for Slimy and Bessy.

Rustin listened carefully but didn't comment.

"What do you know about dimensional faults?" I asked the ghost witch.

"Not much. I don't think anybody knows all that much. It's a gray area in the Universe."

Sebille set tea in front of each of us. I looked up to find Sadie peering down at me from Sebille's shoulder. The little critter blinked and seemed to smile, her black lips curving upward to show me a lot of white teeth and two tiny fangs.

She really was cute.

"Thanks, Sebille," I said.

Rustin nodded in agreement. "This smells delicious."

Sebille returned to grab her own tea, and Rustin continued. "The PTBs are tied to the individual dimensions, as you know. One *Power That Be* is assigned to each one. And when dimensional magics go wonky, there are jurisdictional issues that need to be worked out."

"What does that mean?" Sebille asked, sliding into the last chair with her tea.

"If this is what Madeline thinks it is, there's a fold in the dimensions. When a plane folds, it partially encompasses another dimension. The two basically share the same space. That shared area creates a problem of jurisdictional management that affects everything from, who enforces Universal Laws, to how artifacts are managed and controlled." He gave me a meaningful glance.

"Is that why Madeline says she'll only give me two days to get Slimy and Bessy out of there?"

"It might be. Though, I've heard the spell to snip a wrinkle is complex. Only a really experienced witch can perform it. She might need every bit of that time to write the spell. And/or she's trying to fix the issue before the other affected PTB finds out about it. That would be the simplest thing for everybody."

I thought about the face of the person on the ladder and the cowbell I'd pulled off Bessy and asked, "When the two dimensions are sharing space, is it possible to see only part of an object in that space?"

Rustin nodded. "It's called spacial bleed through. It's a pretty common, though short-lived phenomena." He frowned.

"What is it?" I asked.

Rustin shrugged. "Madeline might want to minimize this wrinkle for another reason. She'd never admit this to you but..." He hesitated as if trying to decide whether to go on.

"But what?" Sebille asked.

"There's another problem. A couple of PTBs have gone missing. And others, not many, but enough to be concerning, have been compromised."

I thought about the *Power That Be* who we'd faced off with not that long ago. He'd definitely been compromised, and when we'd confronted him, he'd turned into a giant stink bug and shot stinky goo at us. I shuddered violently at the memory. "The thing is, I don't know if I can spring the frog and cow that fast. I have no idea how to accomplish it," I told Rustin.

I looked up into Rustin's blue eyes. "She told me it's never been done. That there was no way I could find Slimy and bring him back." I sniffed, appalled to feel tears burning my eyes.

Rustin stared at me for a long moment. Then he nodded. "She's probably right."

I stiffened, despair turning my lips downward.

But Rustin went on. "It probably hasn't ever been done." Then he grinned and the spiders crawling around in my stomach stilled. "But that will only make it sweeter when we manage to do it."

"What are you thinking?" Sebille asked. Sadie scampered over her shoulder, across the back of her neck and over the other shoulder. The little creature flapped her small wings as if trying to fly and burped tiny clouds of multi-hued smoke. Between burps, she chittered softly, her whole demeanor one of happiness and excitement.

I could see why Sebille was so captivated by her.

Rustin glanced around. "Where's Hobs?"

His question brought Maude's strange statement back to me. "He's around here someplace." I narrowed my gaze on the ghost witch. "Maude mentioned Hobs too. What are you two thinking?"

Rustin shook his head. "Nobody ever knows what Maude's thinking." He smiled. "But I was thinking that hobgoblins are really good at inter-dimensional travel."

I had a head-smack moment. "Of course!"

Sebille reached up and gave Sadie her palm, lowering the little creature to the tabletop and smiling as she took off running, circling enthusiastically around Rustin and my teacups. "You're thinking he could travel across the wrinkle and grab Slimy?"

Rustin nodded. "I'm not sure he's got the magical mojo to pull the cow over with him. But he should be able to manage the frog bus, no problem."

I grinned at the old name we'd had for Mr. Slimy, when he'd been the vehicle that allowed Rustin to exist after his body had been stolen from him. "I'll see if I can find him."

Sebille scooped up the tiny lizard, inadvertently sending a fragrant puff of smoke into the air as she carefully wrapped her fingers around the slender, five-inch-long reptile. "We're going to need a lot of frosted brownies to keep him in line."

Sebille was right. Once we took Hobs to a working farm, he was going to get himself into all kinds of mischief. "I'll bring Wicked too. Hopefully, he can help us keep the hobgoblin in line."

Famous last words, best-laid plans, and good intentions. Shame on me for thinking I had a handle on any of them. I needed someone to smack the idea right out of me whenever I'm tempted to develop any of the above-mentioned things.

Or, I could just wait until fate and reality poked me in the eye, and drove my hopes and dreams right out of my mind on a wave of irritation and pain.

It shouldn't take long.

6

AGAIN!

*T*hank the goddess the rain had stopped and the ground had mostly dried out as the sun and wind did their jobs to put things back to rights.

Mr. Wicked bounced over the bumpy pasture ground, happily batting at anything that moved, whether wind-blown or spurred by survival instincts after spotting us trudging along behind the cat.

Hobs rode on Rustin's shoulders, his expressive face filled with delight and his nostrils flaring to take in the dubious fragrance of the post-torrential-rain farm experience.

Without warning, Hobs jumped to his feet and leaped over Rustin's head, landing beside Wicked and mimicking his bug-hunting antics.

I grinned despite myself.

"Those two were made for each other," Rustin said. I glanced his way to find him smiling too.

There was no happiness of any kind being exuded by the third member of our little group. In fact, in direct contrast to our enjoyment of the day and the moment, much harrumphing was going on right behind us.

I turned to find Sebille, her long, freckled face glowing pink with anger and folded into a glower of Sebille-like proportions. She was carefully picking her way across the bumpy and occasionally water-filled pocks that made up the pasture's surface. The Sprite was mad that Lea had canceled at the last minute and Rustin had shamed her into joining us. She was mad about the mud, about the wind, about the bugs, the smell, the animals, the fact that tooth-paste was twenty cents more expensive than last week. Basically, she was mad about everything there was to be mad about.

In a rare concession to practicality over fashion, Sebille had donned canvas coveralls that made her look like a car mechanic and wore sneakers rather than her usual glossy red Wicked Witch of the West shoes.

The sneakers were red. Of course. And, at the moment, one of them was dark with water and mud. The cuffs of her coveralls were stiff with muck.

Apparently, Sebille wasn't having much luck avoiding the small amount of water still left on the ground. I pressed my lips together so I wouldn't smile at her discomfort.

Seeing the Sprite so discomfited over a bit of nature was a delightful irony since her kind is supposed to be at their most comfortable cradled in Mother Nature's arms.

Unlike her family, the City Sprite, as I called her, would rather embrace her favorite television shows on a sixty-inch flat-screen TV and eat carry-out tacos than snuggle up to a vibrant green plant under a great, blue sky.

Never had my favorite moniker for my assistant seemed more appropriate.

"Where did Slimy disappear?" Rustin asked after several minutes of walking.

"Oh." I'd been so fixated on my cat and the hobgoblin, and then Sebille's reaction to being forced to embrace nature, that I'd almost forgotten what we were there for. "In that barn over there."

Sebille stopped beside me, her iridescent green gaze going wide as she took in the ramshackle building. "That doesn't look safe."

"It's perfectly safe," I assured her, before realizing that wasn't entirely true. "Structure-wise," I amended. "Dimensional-wrinkle-wise, it's not safe at all."

Sebille rolled her eyes. Which was, unfortunately, her favorite response whenever I opened my mouth and words came out.

The ground rumbled beneath our feet. I jerked to a stop, going very still. "Do you think that's the wrinkle growing?"

Rustin's gaze slid past me, his dark eyebrows lifting at something he was seeing in the distance. "I'm thinking maybe it's because of *that*."

Sebille and I turned to see what he was looking at as the ground continued to vibrate beneath our shoes.

A dark shape thundered in our direction, dust rising in plumes above the ground around it. Horns curved toward the sky on either side of a long head, making the thing look like a...

"Is that a demon?" Sebille asked.

I watched it come, the thunderous beat of its progress throbbing in my chest, the shape was thick, bumpy, and a shiny circle pierced the thing's dark, angry face. I suddenly realized what it was. "Eagle's entrails!" I yelled, starting to turn. "Run!"

Rustin seemed to realize what it was at the same time I did. He yelped something at Sebille and started running, his footsteps so close to mine I think he stepped on the backs of my shoes a couple of times.

I barely noticed. At that point, I was pretty sure there were tiny little wings on my feet. I barely touched down as my legs stretched underneath me, and my shoes unerringly found the smooth patches of earth between the cow bumps.

A long, high-pitched sound inserted itself into my consciousness. I realized after a moment that it was Sebille. She was screeching as she ran, her fire-red braids streaming out behind her as she jetted past both Rustin and me. Sadie stood backward on her shoulder like a reverse figurehead, her slanted eyes wide as she took in the monster racing after us. The rainbow reptile's mouth was moving. She was probably chittering excitedly, but I couldn't hear her over the oncoming thunder of the enormous bull's approach, and the cacophonous pounding of my own heart.

"We need to get to the barn!" I screamed to my friends, even as I comprehended that we'd never make it. Sebille was ten yards ahead of us and flying fast. I realized she would have shifted into fairy form already if she didn't have the little dragon riding her shoulder. But the Sprite wasn't letting that slow her down. I was pretty sure she was tapping into her Fae magics to give her unnatural speed.

"We're never going to outrun it," Rustin yelled.

Sebille half turned her head, her expression filled with terror. "I don't need to outrun the bull. I just need to outrun one of you."

"Ha, ha!" I yelled over the rumble of hooves. "Very funny."

My heart pounded frantically against my ribs. I sucked desperate gulps of air that were making my chest hurt. And my legs burned as if somebody had set fire to my muscles.

I was starting to think I'd drop dead from exhaustion before the bull even got to me.

And still, the barn didn't seem to be getting any closer.

We were doomed!

A shrill cackle stabbed horror through my gasping chest.

The rumbling hooves behind us stuttered, slowed, and finally eased to a halt.

I ran several more steps before I heard the cackle again. Skimming to a stop, I whipped around and saw my worst nightmare turned real.

The bull stood about fifteen yards away, eyes so filled with rage they seemed to glow red in the afternoon sunlight. It was massive, its hairy chest heaving from the efforts of the acre-wide dash to kill and maim us. The thing's head was bigger than I would be in the fetal position, which I was about to drop into as I looked up at Hobs, sitting astride the monster's back, his spidery fingers clasped around the deadly curved horns and his enormous blue eyes wide with excitement.

Wicked bounced over to me, rubbing against my calf and purring as if his best friend hadn't just climbed up onto the devil and asked for a bumpy ride to Hades.

"Bull boogers," I murmured.

"Is that safe?" Rustin asked as if he'd never met the hobgoblin.

"Of course it's not safe," Sebille said from behind us...wayyyyy...behind us. "The hobgoblin's an idiot."

The bull forcefully snorted air through its huge nostrils, tiny droplets of bull snot spraying out to coat the air around its ridiculously enormous head.

The demonic bovine suddenly flew into the air, twisting and bucking and flinging its head down in an attempt to dislodge the intelligence-challenged invader on its back.

Hobs giggled like a maniac, keeping his hold on the horns even as he was flung forward, off the bull's back and whipped through the air above the bull's head like a bad comb-over in the wind.

At the bull's next iteration of the leap, twist, head-fling thing, Hobs made the return trip, his scrawny legs hitting the bull's back with a smack of flesh against flesh.

Hobs cackled again and rode out the exact same string of events for several more seconds before he was finally flung off the bull's back, cartwheeling through the air and hitting the ground with a splat as he landed in a mud-colored puddle.

There was a beat of silence as everyone took stock of the situation and tried to decide what to do. Then Hobs shot up from the watery hole and yelled, "Again!"

The bull's eyes went wide. Its skinny tail whirled

in a desperate circle, and then the big bovine whipped around and made a run for it, hooves pounding the earth in full retreat.

"Slug slobber," Hobs lamented.

I groaned, holding my side as the stitch I hadn't noticed under a wash of panic-laced adrenaline tried to cut me in half. "Hobs, you're going to be the death of me."

Rustin chuckled. "In his defense, he did defuse the situation."

I shook my head, pressing a hand into my side.

Chirping noises emerged from Sebille's shoulder. A soft whirring noise followed.

Sebille gasped.

I looked up to find Sadie dancing on the air in front of Hobs, tiny wings moving so fast I couldn't see them above her small body. She was chittering happily as she dipped, whirled, and danced from side to side in front of Hobs' delighted face, clearly telling him a story.

"She's flying." Sebille wailed as if announcing the end of the world.

"It's what dragons do," I told Sebille, chuckling at her expression.

"I know, but..."

"Let's go," Rustin said. "We're running out of daylight, and I assume the light isn't that great in the barn."

"Nothing's that great in the barn," I groused.

We started off toward the sagging structure again. I'd like to report that my steps were faster with the knowledge that there was an enraged bull somewhere in the pasture where we walked.

Unfortunately, I was already hurting and weary.

And I still had a frog and a cow to find.

7

FAINTING COUCH FOR ONE PLEASE

I shoved at the big, ramshackle door blocking the entrance to the barn. It creaked and whined against the metal track and then finally gave way with a shriek.

The interior of the place was almost as dim as it had been when I'd been there during a rainstorm. The musty smell of old hay, sour wood, and moldy dirt hadn't changed either.

But a quick glance toward the cow paddock had me narrowing my gaze in speculation.

"What's wrong?" Rustin asked.

"I'm pretty sure there were more cows there yesterday."

He shrugged. "Maybe they're out to pasture."

Sebille was keeping a careful eye on Sadie as the little dragon whirred and spun on the air nearby, clearly enjoying her newly discovered flying ability.

"Where'd you lose the frog bus?" Rustin asked, glancing calmly around.

I swung an arm toward the ladder leading to the loft. "Under that ladder there."

"What ladder?"

I nearly rolled my eyes. "You're such a man sometimes," I groused. "That ladder right th..." I felt my blue eyes widen. "Oh." The ladder was gone. I started toward the area where it had been. The hayloft looked shorter than I remembered too.

Rustin put a restraining hand on my arm, stopping me. "Look at the ground."

I did as directed and frowned, at first not tracking with what I was seeing. The dirt was smooth beneath the loft. I slid my gaze along the ground beneath the loft and noted about a three-foot-wide ribbon of smooth dirt that started inside the cow pen and ended just past where the ladder had been. The air in that space was slightly muzzy, covering everything behind it in a faint white haze. "What is it?"

"The wrinkle," Rustin said, his voice filled with unhappiness. "It's growing."

That can't be good.

"Aaaaaaahhhhhh!"

Yelping in surprise, I swung around at the scream, wishing I had a weapon.

A small, horned animal stood a few feet away, its jaw working busily over something in its mouth.

"What *is* that?" Sebille breathed.

I glanced at my assistant and found her clutching Sadie to her chest with one hand, the other stretched out in front of her spitting green energy.

Rustin laughed. "It's just a goat."

Sebille relaxed slightly, her magic partially dissipating. But I noticed she kept a slight glow of energy around her fingers. Just in case.

I felt smug. Even I knew what a goat was.

Kind of.

"Why is it screaming at us?" I asked.

Rustin shrugged, looking amused. "Who knows. Goats are weird."

"Aaaaaaahhhhhh!"

A small body shot through the door, followed by the sleek gray form of Mr. Wicked. Hobs literally skidded to a stop when he saw the goat, a look of pure glee on his small face. His oversized ears twitched, the strand of light brown hair between them shifting with the movement. "What's that?"

"Goat," Rustin offered.

"Goat," Hobs repeated softly, trying the word on for size. "Cute."

I nodded. "You should leave it alone, Hobs. I think they bite or kick or something."

"As opposed to a Brahma Bull?" Sebille offered snarkily.

I shrugged. Hobs wouldn't listen to me anyway. "We should..."

"Aaaaaaahhhhhh!"

Hobs jumped at the sound, then clapped his hands and cackled. "Aaaaaaahhhhhh!" he responded in a fair imitation of the goat.

The goat's eyes widened, and it fell over onto its side, knobby legs sticking straight out from its body.

I gasped. "He killed it."

Rustin burst into laughter at the look of horror on the hobgoblin's face. "It's okay, Hobs. It's a fainting goat."

When Hobs continued to stare in horror at the little creature, Rustin said. "Really. Watch."

After a few beats, the goat seemed to wake up and quickly climbed to its feet. "Aaaaaaahhhhhh!" it screamed.

Hobs clapped his hands again.

I looked at Rustin. "Anyway..."

He nodded. "Let me see if I can gauge the parameters of the wrinkle. Just give me a minute."

Keeping one eye on the ghost witch, I watched Wicked, Hobs, and the goat scamper playfully around the barn for several minutes while Rustin worked. Their antics kept me chuckling, especially when Hobs tried to climb onto the goat's back to "ride" it bucking bull style. That didn't work out as well as Hobs had expected because, every time he laughed or squealed in delight, the goat toppled over. Out cold.

Sebille and I were laughing hysterically during one such moment when the air lit up with a snap of electrical energy. We whipped around to find Rustin standing about six feet from the area we'd identified as the wrinkle, arms lifted and hands open, palms filled with energy.

In front of him was an area illuminated in soft silvery light. The lit area was roughly the same dimensions as the affected space we'd identified and was irregular, its edges cutting a wavy line in the dirt floor at Rustin's feet.

"Is that the wrinkle?" Sebille asked, still clutching her little dragon close.

Rustin nodded, slowly lowering his hands. "And it's bad news, I'm afraid." He walked over to the magically lit area and crouched down, pointing to a spot in the dirt. "See how the energy is thicker here. That's where the dimensional cross-over is the worst."

"What does that mean?" I asked him, moving closer and eyeing the area. It all looked the same to me.

"The spell I cast coats settled magic more heavily. The thicker coating is on the part of the wrinkle that's been here the longest." He slid his finger along the line. "All of this is new." He stood up and looked at me, his expression dire. "It's moving more quickly than we'd thought. I'm afraid Madeline's assessment of two days was conservative. We need to move quickly. As this thing grows in size, the speed at which it will spread will only increase."

My hopes plunged. "That can't be! I'm already not sure I have enough time to do what I need to do."

Rustin glanced at Hobs, who'd climbed the cow pen wall and was staring at the cows. "There might be one thing we can try..."

"Hello?"

We turned toward the door, where the sunlight from outside formed an aura behind a widely-made man wearing rough clothes and a battered straw hat. He was carrying a dangerous-looking farm gizmo that looked like a giant fork with too many tines. The big man stepped inside, the loss of the sunny aura revealing Farmer Blue. "I didn't know you folks were coming out again." He slid a suspicious look over Rustin and then went wide-eyed at the sight of Sebille.

My assistant scowled at him, her hand sliding protectively over Sadie.

I stepped forward. "Mr. Blue. These are my friends Rustin and Sebille. They're helping me figure out how to get Bessy back."

Blue skimmed a sad look toward the paddock and then back to me. "Lost two more this morning."

I'd been right. There were fewer cows in the

barn. "I'm sorry. We're working as fast as we can." Even to me, my assurances fell flat.

Meanwhile, back at the cow pen, jets of milk had started shooting into the air amid outraged mooing sounds. And there was cackling.

Farmer Blue started to glance that way. I stepped in front of him, motioning to Rustin behind my back to retrieve the naughty hobgoblin.

"Do you know what's going on?" Blue asked. "Is somebody stealing them?"

I really wished it were that simple. I didn't know quite what to say. The Blues seemed to understand that magic was real...or at least *he* did. Mrs. Blue appeared to be in denial. But that didn't mean they'd comprehend, or be comfortable in the knowledge that a dimensional wrinkle was a "thing".

"Hobs!" Rustin whispered harshly.

I struggled for something to distract the farmer. My mind was blank.

Cackling noises sifted from the paddock area. Rustin gasped and jumped back. I could only assume Hobs had hit him with a burst of milk. My jaw tightened and I felt all the color leeching from my face. I was going to kill the hobgoblin.

"You're a Troll," Sebille said, surprising everybody.

Blue didn't flinch, exactly, but his body language changed. He pulled himself straighter, his jaw went taut. "Yes'm. Third generation Land Troll."

She nodded. "You have any Bridgies in your gene pool?"

Blue's frown was one of thoughtfulness rather than displeasure. "Great Great Grampa Blue. He held the North Street Bridge for a century or more. Best Bridge Troll in these parts."

There was a scuffle behind me, and Rustin reappeared, a squiggly hobgoblin under one arm. Hobs was laughing, and Rustin's face was covered in milk.

Farmer Blue eyed the pair of them, his gaze narrowing.

"Then you understand dimensional abnormalities?" Sebille said.

I finally saw where the Sprite was taking him. Unbeknownst to humans, bridges often served more than one dimension as portals. One bridge in a key location can serve as many as five different dimensions. As a result, Bridge Trolls become adept at managing interdimensional traffic, as well as the intricacies of dimensional weirdness.

Blue nodded, his eyes narrowing with understanding. "You think this here's a dimensional fault?" He eyed the shimmering wall of magic Rustin had created.

"A wrinkle," Rustin corrected. "And it's moving fast. My recommendation is that you move your animals to a spot out of the current trajectory to limit your losses."

Blue's gaze turned sad. "Bessy's gone?"

I knew what he was asking. Ignoring the naysaying of both Madeline and Rustin, I shook my head. "I'm not going to let that happen, Farmer Blue. I promised I'd get her back, and I intend to do just that." I could feel Rustin's disapproving glare on my back, but I ignored him. "It *is* a good idea to move your animals, though, before you lose any more."

Blue nodded. "I'll do that. Thank ya much, Naida keeper. We 'preciate yore kindness."

The sadness on his craggy face was nearly my undoing. It was clear to me that Blue cared a lot about his animals. I suddenly felt guilty for being motivated as much by Slimy's disappearance as I was by the loss of his cows. But then I realized there was no shame in that. I felt the same way he did about losing my little green friend.

"I'll just take Adelaide home with me then."

We all blinked in confusion.

"Adelaide?" I asked.

He pointed a thick finger at the goat. "She's got a hidey-hole in the garage, but she likes visitin' with the cows."

"She's a hoot," I told him, grinning.

He chuckled. "She is that. It's time for her ta get her ration of grain. That's why she's screamin'." He moved toward the goat, hand outstretched. He'd produced a short rope with a clasp on one end from somewhere. Probably from one of the many over-sized pockets in his overalls. "Here, Sissy, Sissy."

Adelaide took a step forward, looking as if she might listen, then lifted her gaze to the giant fork he held in his hand.

Blue expelled air. "I forgot. Addie's afeared of pitchforks. We got her from a guy who liked ta chase her with a fork ta stop her screamin'."

I frowned, thinking that *some* people didn't deserve to have furry friends.

When Blue moved to set the pitchfork on the dusty ground, The goat jumped away and, with a final scream of unhappiness, dodged around him and ran right for the shimmering magic below the hayloft.

A chorus of screams didn't stop her and, unfortunately, she didn't faint at the sound. She dove right through the magic and disappeared.

"No!" Farmer Blue said, running forward as if he was thinking about going after her.

Rustin grabbed his arm, stopping him just in time.

A whir of movement and a low, gray form flew past as I reached for the distraught farmer.

And before I could stop them, Wicked and Hobs followed the goat through the wall.

8

INTO WONDERLAND

I lost my mind. In full out panic mode, I dove after them, my hand plunging through the wall a second too late in an attempt to grab Mr. Wicked's sleek, too-fast form.

Sebille and Rustin both screamed my name and I stopped, though it just about killed me to do it. Tears burned my eyes. "Wicked!" I shrieked, sounding like a crazy lady. "Hobs!"

I started to straighten, tugging on my hand.

The magic wouldn't release it.

"Get away from the wrinkle, Naida," Rustin said, moving closer and wrapping his hand around my arm. His fingers slipped right through my flesh and I looked up into his face to see his eyes widening, his gaze sliding to the insubstantial hand. "Oh, oh," he said.

"What's going on?" I asked, trying to yank free

again, but not having any better luck the second time.

"I think I've used up all my energy stores," Rustin said as his entire body blipped and went slightly see-through.

Sebille looked at him with surprise, then glanced down at Sadie. "He needs to let his physical body go for a while."

I sighed. Of course he did. What else could go wrong? I jerked my hand again and then braced myself against the floor as Farmer Blue came over to help.

"I'm gonna grab ya around yore waist, young lady. Don't think I'm bein' over-friendly."

I would have laughed at the idea if I wasn't so devastated. "It's okay. Thank you."

He nodded, wrapped the promised arm around my waist, and tugged as hard as he could, just about tearing me in two as the magic held onto me.

Finally, when I thought he was going to literally split me in half, I yelled for him to stop.

I glanced at Rustin. "Can you make this let me go?"

He nodded, lifted his hands, and disappeared.

Sebille gave a little yelp as Sadie rose out of her grip, her colorful form bending and twisting as if from pain, and then disappeared with a soft plop and a wisp of multi-hued energy.

The magic tugged me closer and real panic set in. I was sunk into it up to my shoulder. "Sebille...?"

She forced her worried gaze to me. "What?" Her tone was angry, and I knew she was worried about Rustin and Sadie.

"I think I'm..."

I never got a chance to finish the thought. The energy gave one more small tug, as if testing the waters, and then yanked me completely through the wall. Energy stung my skin, biting me like a thousand angry bees. The ground changed shape beneath my feet. I stumbled forward, the momentum of my fall taking me several feet past the sizzling wall of energy.

I slammed up against a tree. Fortunately, my hands smacking hard against the smooth bark kept me from hitting the pinkish surface with my nose.

Falling to my knees, I struggled to draw air. My chest tightened, my lungs unable to expand and my throat swollen so that air couldn't make it in or out. For one terrifying moment, I thought I was going to suffocate, but the symptoms began to ease after a moment, and I pulled a thin stream of air into my lungs. Not enough for comfort. But enough to keep me from passing out.

I rolled over to my backside and leaned against the tree as an array of things sifted through my mind.

The breathing problem slowly abated.

The air burned my nostrils and tasted bitter on my tongue. I thought maybe something toxic was burning nearby, but I saw no smoke and no flame.

With breath came an awareness of smell.

A horrible smell.

It was sour and putrid and...familiar. I grimaced down at my hands and my gaze flew to the shimmering wall of energy a mere ten feet away.

There was a perfect handprint in the slimy, aromatic cow patty just inside the wall.

"Ergh!" I slammed my palm onto the sharp-edged, yellow-green grass and rubbed hard. The blades scratched my skin and did little to remove the cow manure from my hand.

I shoved to my feet, dizziness making me stop and double over, breathing through the vertigo caused by standing too fast.

What's wrong with me?

Maybe I've been poisoned by the manure, I thought, grimacing.

I'd certainly been repulsed by it.

The energy of the wall sizzled and snapped, but the sound was starting to fade. The shimmering barrier was growing fainter.

It was going away!

If it disappeared, I'd never find my way back to it. In pure desperation, I ran toward the wall and threw myself at it.

It was like hitting a bolt of lightning.

The energy flared against my skin, spitting angrily, and biting me like a million angry hornets, then it shoved me back with such force my feet left the ground and I flew backward.

I smacked against the grass again and skidded until I hit longer vegetation, which slowed me to a stop after a few more feet.

I lay there groaning, the soft sound of birds and bugs sifting through my mind.

I tried to tug my thoughts into some kind of order and get my limbs to work again. When I thought I'd pushed the dizziness back enough to move, I attempted to push myself upright.

My hand splashed into cool liquid.

I turned my head and peered through the tall grass, seeing the silvery sparkle of a body of water not five feet away.

A pond.

I could wash the cow feces off my hand!

A sense of calm came over me at the sight. It was so pretty. So inherently harmless. What had I been worried about? Why had I stressed being yanked into that dimension?

Wait? What was that terrible smell?

The long grasses rustled.

An aggressive snort filled the air.

And a pair of fierce, red eyes appeared between the moist strands of pond grass.

Pickled pond patties! I turned and started to run as

the bull burst from the grass, head down and intention clear.

I was so infused with adrenaline when the massive head barreled into my backside I barely felt the pain. I was flying through the air, high above the pretty, sparkling pond, before I even realized I'd been hit.

I splashed down at the far end of the small pond, sinking into black, smelly sludge when I landed. I shoved at the muck but my hands just sank deeper, sliding over the snot-like surface and nearly sending me to my back in the nasty stuff. Panicking as my mind started to manufacture all the gross and treacherous stuff that might be living in the muck, I scrambled upward, pulling a few rarely-used muscles in the effort.

I stood there looking at the stinky mud coating my arms up to my elbows and my legs up to my calves. I didn't even want to think about what my backside looked like.

"Ergh!" I groaned, flinging mud off my hands with a few hearty shakes. The black goo hit the water all around me with soft splatting sounds.

A not-too-distant snort had my head whipping up as I remembered the still-present danger standing by the pond. From a safe distance, the bull's gaze looked less hostile and more confused. He was no doubt wondering how he'd gotten there.

He wasn't alone in that. "Shoo! Go away. If you're not going to be nice, you're on your own."

The big, stinky menace snorted again, stomped a massive hoof on the soft ground near the pond, and then turned away and started galloping.

"Good riddance," I muttered, wiping my hands on the front of my jeans. I tried to step out of the pond, but my sneaker was stuck in the mire. I tugged harder and felt the shoe slipping off my foot. "Duck digits!" I exclaimed, reaching the end of my patience. I finally managed to tug my sneaker out, holding it away from my body as it dripped black goo.

Impatience made my stomach tight. I had a frog, a cow, a cat, and a hobgoblin to find. I sighed. "Oh, and a goat," I told myself aloud. "The list just keeps growing."

I peered off into the distance where the bull had gone. "I'm leaving you here," I shouted after the retreating bull.

Rinsing my hands and arms in the water as best I could, I noticed that it was thicker than it should have been. It was also gray rather than clear or mud-colored. I pushed concern aside, figuring the pond was silty from me disturbing the muck around the edge. When I'd cleaned up as best I could, I straightened to look around for the first time. My eyes widened as I took in my surroundings. I'm not sure what I'd been anticipating, but whatever it was, the reality wasn't anywhere close to my expectations.

The pond water that I'd thought was gray was actually silver. I stared down at it, hoping I hadn't just washed my arms in some kind of molten metal, like Mercury or Silver. That was what it looked like. The trees which overhung the pond had pinkish bark. The knots along the trunk and branches were a darker pink that looked like purple polka dots from a distance.

The leaves of the trees were white, silver really, but they looked white in the sun.

I glanced toward the sky, realizing the sun was hotter than it should have been. My eyebrows climbed into my hairline. I was looking at two large, yellow globes of light and heat.

Two suns.

Okay. I'd definitely landed in Wonderland. I just hoped I'd find a helpful mad hatter to show me around the place.

"It's about time you got here."

I jerked spastically at the voice, my gaze sliding around the pond and seeing nobody.

"Hello?" the voice said, dripping with sarcasm. "Down here."

I scoured the area around my feet with a wide gaze, expecting to see a talking turtle or a conversing carp.

I didn't see him at first. He was just a pair of bulging black eyes nestled amongst the lily pads. Or, I guessed they were lilies. They had tiger stripes and oversized stigma at the centers that were a neon orange.

I narrowed my gaze on the frog. "Mr. Slimy? Is that you?"

The frog swam out of the flowers, hopping out of the water and landing on the warmed, flat surface of a rock which was half-buried in the muck. "Does a bull stink?"

"Yes," I said, relief swamping me. "A bull definitely stinks."

I crouched down and looked him over. He didn't look injured, but I thought he might have grown some since I'd last seen him.

"It's this water. Everything around it and inside it is bigger. You should see the garter snake that lives under that rock over there. He's huge and he's been looking at me like I'm dinner." The frog eyed my backside. "You might want to keep your butt out of this water too."

"Har de har," I told him.

I was shocked by the idea that he could have grown. It had only been a few hours, hadn't it? How was that possible?

"How do I know?" he responded saucily. "It just is."

I fell backward onto my recently insulted butt and shook my head. "I'm dreaming, that's it. I hit my head on a rock when the bull launched me and I'm still asleep." I dug a rock out from under my mud-caked butt and flung it across the water. It skipped five times and then stopped, sitting on top of the thick silver water before sinking slowly out of view.

I bit the inside of my lip. "I'm not liking this water one bit."

Slimy's pudgy green form rippled as if he'd shrugged. "It's not so bad. But I'm pretty sure I've been hearing the music from Jaws. I think something lives at the bottom. Something we probably don't want to meet."

I snatched him up and crab-walked away from the silvery liquid. "Okay, let's get out of here."

"Good, the frog said. I can't wait to get home."

"Not so fast, grasshopper," I said.

Slimy got excited, hopping up and giving a happy little croak. "Where? I'm starving."

"It was a movie reference," I narrowed my gaze at him. "How can you be hungry? You're surrounded by bugs and stuff. You should be fat and happy right now."

Well, truth be told, he did have the fat part down.

"No fat-shaming. It's mean."

Says the frog who just told me I had a big butt, I thought.

"Well, to be fair," he said, "I merely insinuated it."

I sighed. I so was not going to like this new mind-reading skill of the frog's. Hopefully, it would go away when we got back.

"*You* don't like it? What about *me*? It's a dark and vastly empty place inside your head."

"Hey!"

He chuckled, making me smile. "We can't go home just yet. Mr. Wicked and Hobs are here somewhere, and Adelaide and Bessy."

"Adelaide and Bessy?"

"A fainting goat and the cow we were hired to find."

"We were hired to find a cow?"

"Yeah, that's why we were in the barn when you got caught inside the wrinkle and ended up here. Haven't you been paying attention?"

"Barn? What barn?" Slimy asked.

Well, that answered that question. I looked him over carefully, wondering if he'd hit his head when he came through the wrinkle. He looked like my Mr. Slimy. Same squishy green form. Same blank black eyes.

"Hey!" the frog objected. *Trickle, trickle.*

I sighed. "Same incontinence problems."

"I'm not incontinent. Frogs pee where and when they want to. We resist the pressure to conform."

"We'll see how long you resist when I make you start wearing diapers."

I felt his outrage in the trembling of his body.

"Yeah. So there."

Trickle, trickle.

"Aaaaaahhhhh! You did that on purpose."

He chuckled happily. "Never threaten a frog you're holding in your hand. We have resources."

"Four words, frog. Teeny, tiny amphibian diapers," I set him on the ground and quickly rinsed my hands in the silvery water. The surface rippled nearby and something long broke through the ripples, a slanted pair of yellow eyes peering with dangerous hostility as I yanked my hands from the pond. "It's time to go."

We set off away from the pond, me trying to search the ground for tracks but continually getting distracted by the green birds in the trees above my head. Or the pale orange, deer-like creatures that had fangs and long tails like panthers. It didn't take long for the heat of the double suns to turn me into a sweaty, uncomfortable wreck.

My feet were sore, the heated mud on my jeans was giving off a terrible stench, and my stomach was so empty it hurt.

I had no idea how long I'd been there, but I was pretty sure I'd missed lunch and maybe dinner. I was going to have to find something to eat pretty soon.

"I think we're walking in circles," sayeth the frog.

Sighing, I scrubbed my sweaty forehead with the back of one hand. "It's highly probable. I have no sense of direction, and I'm in a world where every-thing looks the same." I didn't know if that was precisely true. Everything might just look the same because I was going in circles.

I dropped onto a large rock I was pretty sure I'd seen before and looked into the distance toward a spiky horizon of golden peaks that were also hauntingly familiar. Glancing up at the double suns, I realized they were lower in the purplish sky. "I think it's getting late. What happens here at night?" I asked Slimy.

He stared into the distance, throat flaring and subsiding. He was either in deep thought, or his tiny little brain had seized up.

"Again with the innuendo about me having an empty head," he lamented.

"Hey, you did it to me first."

"Yeah? And I'm also not the boss of you."

I rolled my eyes, realizing I was channeling Sebille. "Okay, listen. I get it. You're snarky. I'm snarky. Everybody's snarky. But two snarks do not make a right…"

Slimy blinked at me, looking perplexed.

"Or something like that. We need to start working together, or we're never going to find Wicked…" The thought clogged my throat and made my eyes burn under a wash of unwelcome tears. I took a shaky breath. "I need to find him and Hobs. You want that, right?"

The frog sighed. "Of course. I've been wracking my brain trying to figure out where they might be."

I clamped down on a snarky rejoinder about his wracked brain and sniffled, dragging my sleeve under my nose. "Okay. Good. Have you come up with anything? Because I'm blanking here."

"No. Sorry."

He really did sound sorry, so I tightened my jaw against the desire to yell. "Okay. Well, I guess we'd better find a spot to spend the night. Then I need to find something to eat." Slimy had been snatching bugs as we traveled, so I didn't need to worry about him. Except that he probably needed water. "Do you smell water anywhere?" I asked.

"Yes. It's not far. That would be a good place to sleep for the night."

I nodded, agreeing but too tired and emotionally drained to even tell him so. "Lead the way."

Slimy hit the glossy water as soon as we found it, swimming happily around before finding a floating log and settling down on top of it for the night. I was dying of thirst myself but I was about half afraid of drinking the thick, silvery stuff.

So to distract myself from my thirst, I set about gathering leaves for a bed in the protective shadow of two large rocks, beneath a pink and purple polka-dotted tree in case it rained. Or, heck, snowed. Who knew what the atmosphere of the current dimension was like?

A suitable resting place configured, I set off to find something to eat. In desperation, I sent my seeking energies out, hoping maybe to find a waffle maker artifact that came complete with already cooked waffles.

Hey, a girl can dream.

To my vast surprise, there was a distant chime of discovery. I headed in the direction it had sounded, finding nothing that looked like an artifact. "False find," I murmured unhappily.

I hadn't gone far when I found a tree that looked different from the water-loving trees around the ponds. It was shorter, its branches spreading out instead of up, and had brown bark that wasn't smooth and silvery green leaves. Nestled within the leaves were what I assumed could only be pieces of fruit. The fruit was orange, oval in shape, and had bumpy skin. I picked one and smelled it hopefully. It smelled sort of like an orange, but when I peeled it, the meat was smooth like an apple. I gave it a tentative lick and found it sweet and juicy.

I waited a few minutes and, when it didn't disintegrate my stomach or make me froth at the mouth, I picked several of the strange fruits and carried them back to my leafy bed.

They were delicious, the meat of the fruit was so juicy it alleviated my thirst while it filled my stomach. I tried not to think of the fact that they could be poisonous as I consumed the fourth one. If I didn't eat or drink, I was going to die anyway so I told myself it was worth the risk.

As night fell and the nocturnal world woke and started to communicate through the dark, singing, croaking, rustling, and screaming into the night, I thought I was much more likely to die from something hungry beyond my little nest than I was from the fruit.

I tugged my coat closer around me and settled in, trying not to think of what might have happened to my friends after they came through the wrinkle.

I fell asleep to the last orange stain of twilight painting the sky. Even the belch of the bullfrogs and the occasional splash of something on the move beneath the weird water couldn't keep me from falling into a deep, dreamless sleep.

9

DANG HIS WRINKLED SOUL

I didn't open my eyes when I first woke up. I'd slept deeply when I'd slept, but I'd woken up several times throughout the night in response to strange noises. The broken sleep pattern had left me tired, despite the fact that the sun was already bright and hot, and I was pretty sure it was late morning.

It was the prickles between my shoulder blades that finally inspired me to open my eyes. And when I did, I jolted upward with a shriek, startling the man standing a few feet away, his eyes hidden behind a strange-looking pair of glasses. "Ya," he said by way of greeting. "Halfun?"

I scrambled backward until I came up against the rocks guarding my back. My mind still muzzy from sleep, it took me a minute to process the strange question. "What?"

His lips curved up in the corners.

Despite my pounding heart and the shortness of breath that came with panic, I took a beat to appreciate the strong nose, square chin and thick cap of...green...hair. "Hello."

He nodded. "Ya."

He was either a very agreeable person, or he was speaking to me in a different language.

Just great.

I pushed slowly to my feet.

He looked me over, his eyes narrowing at my muddied and rumpled state. Then his gaze found the orange peels from my meal the night before and the smile dropped away. He lifted his gaze, and I was pretty sure it would be filled with horror if I could see it behind the triangular blue glasses. But the lenses were too dark for me to see his eyes.

"What's wrong? Is that fruit poisonous?"

The man didn't answer. Instead, he hurried away from me and I followed. He walked briskly, with really long strides that seemed almost comical.

He covered the distance to the fruit tree very quickly, and I had to almost run to keep up. When he got there, he raced around the tree, carefully searching the ground underneath it. Then he stepped back and looked up at the sky, tugging the glasses off his face and spinning in a fast circle before turning back to me. "It is very dangerous to take the Seer's gloff."

"Gloff?" I shook my head. "I'm sorry. I don't know who the Seer is. I was hungry and..."

He shook his head, hurrying toward me.

I flinched back, lifting my piddly fists as if to punch him.

He looked shocked. Then amused. "You would strike me?"

"If you try to...erm...strike me first."

The man frowned, replaced the glasses, and turned away, striding back to the pond as quickly as he'd come. I thought he was going to leave but he stopped by my little nest and grabbed up all the peels, then plucked some kind of long stick with a small metal head from where it had been leaning against a tree and began to dig in the soft soil near the pond.

I watched him carefully, not sure if I was more worried about the shovel-like implement he was using, or the concern he clearly had about the Seer guy.

I finally decided the unknown and unseen was worse than the shovel, which he seemed only inclined to use to bury my peels. "Who is the Seer and why are you so afraid?"

He stopped digging and looked at me, his expression filled with astonishment. "You come from space?"

When I frowned, he pointed toward the sky. "Space?"

I shook my head. Then I realized I kind of did come from space. "Another dimension, actually. I'm looking for my frie..."

"Dimension?" He glanced in the direction Slimy and I had come and frowned. "No."

Misunderstanding, I hurried to assure him it was true. "No, really. There's a wrinkle between your dimension and mine. I fell into it and I'm looking for my friends. They also fell through it by accident."

He was staring at me as if I'd lost my mind. Clearly, he had no clue about the wrinkle. Which might be good or bad. I tried another tack. "I'm looking for a gray cat. He'd be with a little guy with big ears and big feet. And there's a goat and a cow too. Have you seen them?"

He stared at me for another long moment and then turned away, stomping on the dirt he'd covered the peels with. He mopped his brow with a striped cloth he tugged from his back pocket and gave the sky one last look. "Come." He turned away and started toward the tree line on the far side of the pond.

"Um..."

He turned but didn't stop walking. "Come. I help."

He help. Okay. I could live with that. Probably. "I just need to get my frog..." Realizing how that probably sounded, I sighed. My life was a cartoon. And I was the character that the other cartoon characters liked to beat on all the time.

"Slimy," I whispered harshly.

No answer.

"Slimy, come on. I found somebody to help."

Nothing.

My helper turned around, walking backward as he motioned for me to follow. "Come!"

I expelled a frustrated breath. "Okay. Stay here. I'm going to check out the lay of the land and come back for you in a little bit."

I walked reluctantly away, casting worried glances back toward the pond several times until I stepped into the trees and lost sight of it. Fighting worry, I told myself I was just leaving a frog in a pond. Hardly a dire situation.

I mean, I wasn't leaving him in the kitchen of a French restaurant or anything.

Presumably, his spindly, crooked little legs were safe in the pond.

As safe as mine were, anyway.

Following my new friend through the woods, which seemed to be getting darker and creepier by the moment, I considered that Slimy might be the smarter one of the two of us.

Then the trees suddenly gave way, and the path led out into a vibrantly green strip of open land.

I looked down on an entire city.

Two minutes from where I'd spent the night.

"Don't tell me I was this close to civilization, and I slept on a bunch of leaves on the ground last night."

He grinned. "Welcome to Wilshire Plex."

Alrighty then.

The double suns beat down on us as my new friend and I walked along narrow streets made of sparkling cobblestones in various shades of gray and brown. The streets were spotless as if nobody ever used them, and I saw no vehicles, pack animals, or carrying contrivances of any kind. Which, of course, made me wonder how people got around.

The buildings were all different heights and shapes, looking like something from outer space. Some tall and rectangular, some short and round, and I even saw one that was like an upside-down triangle. The buildings were all built of stone, but the colors varied from white to orange and even bright green.

It was a singularly unusual place.

"My name is Naida," I told my friend.

He turned to me in surprise, dropping his glasses low on his nose with a shift of his facial muscles and looking at me over them. "Oh. I'm sorry. Walt."

It took me a moment to realize he was giving me his name. "Walt?"

He nodded and I offered him my hand.

He stared at it, perplexed.

After a beat, I pulled it back and wiped it over my jeans with embarrassment. It came away dirtier than before. "Thank you for helping me." Though I wasn't sure what exactly he was helping me with. He hadn't seemed to know anything about Wicked, Hobs, or the farm animals.

Walt nodded briskly. "The Seer will know about your friends," he told me.

"The Seer? I thought we were afraid of him?"

Walt snorted out a laugh.

We stopped in front of a tall, narrow building made of some kind of purple stone or brick. Like everything else I'd seen in the current dimension, the stone sparkled slightly, giving off a magical energy that I felt against my skin.

Walt opened a rounded door with a single narrow window that ran from the top of the door to the bottom. The glass in the door perfectly reflected the nearly cloudless sky, giving nothing away of the building we were about to enter.

He stepped aside, motioning for me to enter.

The smell was the first thing to hit me as my eyes slowly adjusted to the dimmer light inside the building. It smelled like mountain streams, green things, and snow. It also smelled like tacos, though I thought that last was probably a figment of my hungry imagination.

The door closed behind me, shutting off the light, and I blinked. We were still outside. Though it was a far different outside from the one we'd just left.

We stood on an uneven, rocky surface covered in scrub bushes and bent, stunted trees that hung crookedly as if gravity had taken hold of them at a young age and kept a constant downward pull on them as they matured. The air was cool, sweet, and fresh, and in the distance, which was far more distant than I'd have expected given the size of the building, mountain peaks were painted a pure, unblemished white.

"What just happened?" I asked my new friend.

Walt laughed. "The Seer is slightly eccentric. He enjoys living outdoors but prefers to be able to control his environment."

"The ultimate control freak, huh?" I stared around in amazement. "It must take a lot of power to do this."

Walt shrugged. "Seers are powerful creatures."

He moved past me and started along a pathway that wound through the uneven topography of the ground where we walked. I quickly noticed it tracked steadily upward too, the effort of climbing taking its toll on my breathing.

I really needed to do something about getting in

shape. Artifact wrangling was surprisingly more physical than I would have expected. "Where are we going?" I asked Walt.

He turned and gave me a quick smile but didn't respond. I noticed he'd taken the funny glasses off, and his eyes were very bright in the low light.

It seemed like an hour later when I smelled smoke. "Something's burning."

Walt nodded. "The Seer is working. Don't worry. We're almost there."

He must have heard me panting like a water buffalo in the desert. "Oh really," I said. "I was just starting to enjoy the walk."

Walt chuckled. Apparently, he wasn't gullible.

Whistling warthogs! I'd really been hoping to slide that one past him.

We rounded a large outcropping of rock, coming upon a campfire and a tiny, wizened man sitting cross-legged beside it. He wore black robes with wide sleeves that hung down over his hands and puddled around his crossed legs. The hood covered most of his hair and painted shadows across the bulk of his face.

In the glow of the fire, I saw part of what looked like a tarnished watch hanging from a leather tie around his neck, the metal stained dark with soot from the fire.

He didn't look up as we approached, but sat rocking to a beat inside his head, one hand occasionally flinging some kind of dust into the fire. The dust made the fire flare in a variety of colors, and each time it flared, the Seer would stop rocking, focus his gaze carefully on the smoky bloom of color, and then begin rocking again.

Walt motioned me toward the fire. He walked alongside me, so close his arm occasionally bumped against mine. We stopped a couple of feet from the fire and waited.

I had no idea what we were waiting for, but I figured Walt knew. He was the one driving the LaLa-Land bus. I was just a tired and filthy passenger.

Finally, the Seer looked up and I jumped. His eyes were black under a fringe of hair too dark for his heavily lined face. The black encompassed not just the iris's, but the entire surface of his eyes. "You have come far, young one. You are lost."

I certainly couldn't argue with any of that. "I'm looking for my friends."

He nodded. "I have seen them." The wrinkled old man cocked his head. "The one with pointed ears is chaos personified."

Hobs. Relief flared through me "He is. Do you know where they are?"

"Across the magic land, beneath the dual sky, between your hopes and expectations, and above the fear of their loss."

I stared at him for a long moment.

Walt nodded, seeming to think the old man had

actually given us something. "Thank you, great Seer."

The tiny, wrinkled man stared at Walt for an extended beat, and then pointed his scary black eyes back down to the fire, throwing a handful of dust into the flames.

Walt grabbed my arm and led me away, back down the path we'd climbed to see the…erm…Seer.

"What did that mean?" I asked him.

Walt shrugged. "I have no idea. Nobody ever understands what the Seer says."

Frustration twisted in my chest. I clenched my jaw as anger swept through me. "Then why did we come all the way here?"

Walt favored me with a quick glance, his gaze sparking with something that might have been humor. "Because every journey starts with the Seer."

I bit back an angry response. I'd never been good at riddles. And this one, in particular, didn't seem to make any sense at all. But I would have to solve it if I had any hope at all of finding my friends.

Behind me, a soft rumble vibrated the air and I recognized it as laughter.

Apparently, the Seer was a practical jokester.

Dang his wrinkled soul.

It was dark when we came out of the Seer's home. I couldn't believe we'd been gone that long, so I asked Walt.

He glanced up at the sky. "Mid-day aphotic. Come. I'll get you food."

Food! My stomach rumbled hopefully. Then I had a terrible thought. "This isn't going to be pretend food, is it? Because I'm not sure I can take another practical joke like the Seer and keep from strangling somebody."

Walt stopped dead in his tracks and looked at me, wide-eyed and horrified. "Violence? There will be no violence in Plex."

I swallowed hard. *Oops!* "It was just a figure of speech. I wouldn't really strangle anybody."

A woman passing by on the street gasped, her hand rising to her mouth as she gave a little scream and took off running.

"What?" I yelled after her. "I said I *wouldn't* strangle anybody."

Several more screams blared through the darkness around me. Walt grabbed my arm, firmly shoving me ahead of him down the street. "Stop talking before you cause a riot," he whispered harshly.

Man, Plexians were sensitive souls. I clamped my mouth closed and let him herd me down the street, my mind racing. I was going to have to strike out on my own. Coming with Walt had proven to be a waste of time and energy. I was pretty sure at least one of my two days had passed and I was no closer to finding my friends. My situation was quickly coming down to one of two outcomes, neither one palatable. Either Madeline would run out of time and have to close the wrinkle with me in it, dooming me, Mr. Wicked, Hobs, Bessy, and Adelaide to a lifetime in the strange dimension that housed the Seer and green-haired green-eyed Walt, or I'd have to figure out how to stop the wrinkle so I'd have more time to find my friends.

Either way, I couldn't waste any more time in Wilshire Plex. I turned to tell Walt I was leaving. He opened a door and the succulent scent of cooking meat wafted out to tantalize my senses.

"Come. We will eat. And then you will tell me why you are in Plex."

My stomach grumbled violently, and I realized I could wait a tiny bit longer to head out on my own.

10

ACROSS THE MAGIC LAND...

There were just so many of them.

Walts. Waltettas. Waltines. Walteds. Walterinas. Waltys. Of course, those weren't really their names, but they looked so much alike it was weird.

I lost track of the smiles and faces, the helpful hands pushing food at me. I took the food and shoved it in my face, feeling guilty that Mr. Slimy was stuck at that pond, eating bugs and bathing in the sun that I could see through the windows had returned.

Wait...Okay, no guilt for that.

Shaking off the silly thought, I tried to understand the conversation swirling around me.

I gathered from the startling resemblance between them...green hair, dark green eyes, and matching noses and facial structure...that they were all family. There was an older couple, nearly as wizened as the Seer had been. I figured those were Walt's grandparents. The slightly younger couple was undoubtedly his parents.

And the dozen or so female and male Walts of assorted sizes, even down to a tiny baby sleeping in a rocking crib near the table, were no doubt his brothers and sisters.

All I knew for sure was that the food was the best I'd ever eaten and that the conversation was like nothing I'd ever heard before.

Smiling shyly, Walt handed me the platter filled with skewers of moist, spicy meat.

"Thanks," I told him. "Your family is nice. What is that language they're speaking?"

He gave me a strange look. "It is our language."

"How is it that you speak English?"

"English?" He shrugged. "I speak what I hear."

"But," I started to say.

"Would you like some more conchka?" A gentle female voice asked from over my shoulder.

I looked up in surprise, finding Walt's mother offering me a plate of the flavorful spherical objects that looked and tasted like potatoes. I nodded eagerly. "I'd love some. They're delicious."

After I'd helped myself to the offered food, I thanked her. I suddenly realized I could understand everyone around the table.

Walt must have seen the expression on my face because he laughed. "Plexians are hearing learned."

When I still didn't understand, he clarified. "If we hear a language spoken, we can immediately adopt that language. The more we hear it, the better our speech in that language becomes. It's a useful gift."

It would be a very useful gift. "Do you get a lot of different languages passing through Plex?"

He laughed. "You'd be surprised. Now, please, tell us how you came to be here and what you are looking for."

I quickly outlined the wrinkle issue and told them about losing my friends through the shifting barrier. Other than some meaningful glances shared between the elders of the group, they stayed silent, listening to me with rapt attention.

When I'd finished, I looked at Walt, hoping he'd somehow present a magical fix for my problem.

He looked at his parents and grandparents. A lively discussion in a language I didn't recognize ensued. Finally, Walt nodded.

"What's going on?" I asked. "What are they saying?"

But Walt wasn't the one who answered me. It was his grandfather, who truly looked exactly like his grandson, except that his face was covered in deeply etched lines, and his green hair was thinner and peppered with gray. "We have heard of this dimensional shift before." He frowned, leaning over the table and resting his age-speckled forearms on it. "It is our heritage, I'm afraid. Plex was created as a buffer between dimensions. It is our lot to manage such a shift."

Hope flared in my chest. "Then you know how to fix it?"

He sighed. "We did, once upon a time. But the Seers who once foretold of the shifts have long since left. We are helpless against them now. We've lost many miles and hundreds of good people to the treachery of the dimensions."

My heart broke for the people sitting around that long table. They'd lost people. Lots of people to wrinkles like the one I'd come through. My problems suddenly seemed small compared to theirs. "We need to fix this then," I told them. "We need to find a way."

The elder Walts shared looks that told me they'd given up hope. With a sinking feeling in my belly, I realized I was on my own.

I shoved to my feet. "I need to go. Thank you for the meal. It was wonderful."

Walt stood with me, glancing at his parents. They nodded. He reached out and touched my hand. "Wait for me. I'm coming with you. I have an idea of something we can try."

Slimy was sunbathing on a flat rock when we arrived back at the pond. He had no explanation for his silence before and I couldn't help feeling as if he just hadn't wanted to leave. "The nights are short here," the frog said, sliding a bulging gaze toward Walt. "There's more sunlight. I like it."

Walt didn't seem the least surprised by a talking frog. "Sorry to disappoint, but that was just mid-day dark. Darkness falls for full night in about four hours."

I could almost hear Slimy's gears turning. "So, there's *more* darkness here?"

Walt nodded.

Slimy leaped into the pond and swam toward the edge. "Let's blow this kickstand."

"Um..." I said, giving Walt a rueful grin. "Yeah. Let's blow the kickstand."

Walt didn't know enough about Earthly colloquialisms to know how badly Slimy had "blown" that one. He simply turned and started walking. "We'll need to move fast. The border is several hours away by foot. If we hurry, we might make it before fulldark."

We moved in a direction that I thought was away from the spot where I'd come through the wrinkle. But I couldn't be sure, because I was pretty sure I'd walked in circles for a while the night before.

Walt answered my questions about the landscape, animals, and dual suns as we walked. Perched
on my shoulder, Mr. Slimy stayed quiet, only moving
when a hapless bug ventured too close to his deadly
tongue.

The suns seemed to be following us, moving
down the horizon at a pace that made me suspect we
wouldn't quite make it to the border before the twin
orbs were gone.

"How bright is your moon?" I asked. I hadn't
noticed a moon the previous night, when I'd fallen
asleep beside the silver-watered pond, but I'd just
assumed it was hidden by the big tree lumbering
over my makeshift bed.

"Moon?" He shook his head. "We call it fulldark
for a reason."

Gnarled gnat knees! "You mean there's no light at
all?"

"Not out here in the wilderness, no."

As we walked, the place of trees and ponds
slowly transformed into a more desert-like space,
with sandy soil and sinktraps that resembled the
quicksand I was familiar with. I told Walt I'd seen
quicksand before and he nodded.

"Most of the sinktraps have bottoms," he told me.
"But sometimes the bottoms are inaccessible."

In other words, if you fell into one them, you'd
probably die. Not reassuring.

A loud caw, high overhead, had Walt wrenching

his gaze upward. His shoulders tensed and he stopped, pointing toward a rocky crest not too far away. "In there, fast."

I saw a shallow indentation in the rock wall. "In there? Why?"

Walt grabbed my arm and took off running. "Hurry!"

We dove into the shallow cut in the wall just as several large shapes flew overhead, their shadows strangely humanoid as they skimmed across the light brown dirt.

Except for the large, bat-like wings moving on either side of their bodies.

My nose twitched under a smoky scent and magic prickled against my skin. "What...?"

Walt lifted a hand to silence me, his gaze following the flight of the creatures overhead. They flew quickly past, silent except for the soft throb of wings on air. After a moment, he expelled a breath. "I don't think they saw us."

"What were those things?" I asked as Walt left the indentation.

I followed him out, my gaze scouring the sky for signs of the large, winged creatures.

He started off again, quicker than before. "Unfortunately, Plex borders on the demonic dimension. Sometimes they fall into a shift, as you did. If it wasn't for the warning by that Worc, they'd have probably gotten us."

My eyes went round. "Demons?"

He nodded. "The worst kind. Thieves and scavengers. They are without resources when they find themselves stranded here and they have magic, which gives them an edge. They tend to just take whatever they want and not worry about the consequences. The Worc population has been hit especially hard. The demons seem to consider them a delicacy."

I assumed Worcs were birds and that the crow-like caw I'd heard had been the warning he mentioned. "Plexians don't have magic?" I thought sadly of my keeper magics, which had very little or zero use for me in the strange dimension.

Walt shook his head. "Not traditional magics, no. Our gifts are based mostly on feats of engineering and the study of languages."

His words made me think of the Seer's home. "Engineering such as creating a mountainous region inside the Seer's home?"

Walt frowned. "That is purely Seer magic. The Seers guide us in our engineering gifts, but they cannot share their magics." He frowned. "Unfortunately, we're losing even that small gift from them. They've been disappearing, one by one. There are only a very few left now."

"Is that why you've lost the ability to fix the dimensional wrinkle?"

Walt quickly scanned the sky again before

answering my question. "Plex is an integral part of the Universe. We were tasked Millennia ago with the job of keeping the dimensions from sliding. To accomplish this, our Seers were given massive amounts of power." He slid me a gaze filled with meaning. "Power corrupts."

Yes, it did. "They went dark?"

He frowned as if not understanding my reference.

I tried again. "The Seers were more interested in benefitting from their power than they were in doing what the Universe tasked them with doing?"

"Yes."

"Where did they go?" I asked.

Walt looked at me and blinked. "Go?"

"I presume they left Plex somehow. Maybe they went somewhere they could barter with their magics."

He shrugged. I got the impression he didn't want to talk about the missing Seers.

Thinking of Hobs and Wicked, I said, "I need to find my friends before I go back."

He nodded. "There is one at the border who can help with that."

I glanced up at the quickly darkening sky. "How much farther?"

Walt opened his mouth to respond, but never got the chance.

An enormous winged shape dropped silently

from the sky and clamped two black-skinned hands with long, curved claws over his shoulders.

The thirty-foot-wide wings pounded the air and the demon lifted away from the ground, more quickly than I could have imagined carrying that much weight.

"Walt!" I reached for his quickly ascending leg, getting my hands on a bony ankle before he was out of range, and struggled to hold on as the demon's wings pounded the air hard and slow, the movement easily taking him up another foot even with my added weight.

When I still held on, the nasty creature shot forward, ramming me into a spiky tree hard enough to knock me senseless.

I grunted in pain and lost my grip on Walt, falling the rest of the way to the ground.

I struggled to rise, my limbs wobbly and weak. *Walt*! I stared up into the dim light, seeing my new friend's pale face looking resigned and unhappy.

"Fight, Walt!" I screamed. "Don't just hang there!" My voice throbbed with rage. I would have felt guilty about yelling at a man who was clearly helpless and no doubt in agony, but if he didn't fight, he was going to die.

Then I had more immediate problems to deal with. A shadow dropped toward me, and I heard the soughing of enormous wings on the air.

I glanced up just in time to see a wide black face,

red eyes, and a cold smile showing square white teeth. The golden hair curving from a center part around a pair of curved black horns looked strange on the demon, as did the shapely curves of an obviously female creature.

As she plunged out of the sky, claws bent in anticipation of grabbing me, I realized Mr. Slimy had fallen off my shoulder when I'd slammed into the tree.

I couldn't lose him there.

Panic flaring, I dove under the small tree I'd fallen against, hoping the spiky branches would be enough to slow the demon down.

And they would have if the thing hadn't landed a few feet away and come at me on foot.

I scurried around the tree, keeping the trunk between me and the monster as I searched frantically for the frog. "Slimy! Talk to me. Where are you?"

"That bug's too big for me to eat, Naida," Slimy said in a perfectly reasonable voice. "I'd prefer something a bit more my size."

I couldn't help it. I laughed. "That makes two of us." I found him hopping around near a dusty rock, apparently looking for dinner. Nothing got between the frog and his dinner. I could respect that about him. I would have really loved a handful of egg rolls right about then.

Warm air blew over me as I grabbed Slimy. The

whispery sound of feathers brushing against flesh told me the creature had folded her wings. "Come out, come out, wherever you are," she trilled in a husky falsetto that was just wrong.

Cradling the frog in both hands, I backtracked rapidly as the demon stalked me. I was reluctant to turn my back on her to take off running. I was pretty sure she'd catch me quickly anyway, and I didn't relish the idea of claws digging into my back. I'd had nightmares about that whole "claws in the back" thing when I was a kid. I have no idea why. But I did. And the two-inch-long curved claws on the tips of the demon's scaled fingers looked like just the kind of thing to give me new nightmares.

"I have nothing for you. I'm stranded here just like you are," I told the monster in a bid to create a connection that might save my life.

I might as well have saved my breath.

The demon's smile widened. "I don't know about that. It looks to me like you're holding dinner in your hands."

I looked down at Slimy and then back up at her, my mouth falling open in outrage. "You can't eat Mr. Slimy. He's a magical frog."

The demon stopped, her scary red gaze widening. "Magical? How?"

"He talks."

She thought about that for a moment. "Can he make himself bigger?"

"No."

"Can he clone himself?"

"No. He just talks."

She shrugged. "I don't mind if my food talks to me on the way down." The demon moved and she was suddenly on top of me, her hands shoving me backward as her wings came up. "I'll just take my talking dinner now."

She reached for Slimy and I panicked. Without thinking, I shot her with a beam of keeper magics.

The silvery light flared outward, a pulsating beam as wide as my arm, and smacked into her. But instead of pulling her to me as my magics generally did, the energy shoved her away. Hard. Hard enough to send her flying thirty yards to smack up against a large, jagged rock.

The demon crumpled to the ground and collapsed, seemingly unconscious. I didn't wait around to see if she was. I took off running in the direction the demon had taken Walt. I could barely see them in the distant sky, and it was getting dark fast.

I ran faster, using my energy to give me speed. I couldn't shake the feeling that, if I didn't find my friend before morning, there wouldn't be anything left of him to find.

11

BENEATH THE DUAL SKY...

*I*t was so dark. I'd lost sight of Walt and the demon what felt like an hour since. I'd been reduced to stumbling along blindly, hoping I was keeping the same trajectory I'd had before I'd been blinded by the complete and disorienting blackness.

I walked with my hands stretched out in front of me, my ears tuned toward any sound that would mean the return of the demons or any other source of danger or trouble that might be wandering around out there with me.

When one of my feet slipped deeply into a sink trap, I managed to wrench it free and fling myself away from the trap before I fell into it. The experience left me shaken, and I moved more slowly after that, stretching out a foot and feeling ahead of me with every step to make sure I was on solid ground.

It was a slow, tedious process.

My ankle twisted under me and I fell to my knees as agony speared my leg and foot. I was caught in something. From what I could tell by feeling with my fingers, it was a wide crevice in the hard earth. Jerking as hard as I could in an attempt to free my foot, I almost lost the frog, who'd been dozing on my shoulder. My foot came free and I barely caught Slimy before he flew off my shoulder. My heart pounded with fear and frustration. If I lost him in the extreme dark, I'd never find him again until morning. And I wasn't sure I could wait until morning to move forward.

The sense of urgency I'd been feeling since being sucked through the wrinkle had grown to a constant, nerve-stripping demand over the last few hours.

It was as if my inner clock was trying to tell me I was running out of time. But I didn't need a clock to tell me that. I'd slept one night in Plex. I was moving through a second night.

There couldn't be many hours more before Madeline would be forced to close the breach with my friends and me on the wrong side.

A low rumble filled the air. Static electricity bit my skin like a thousand hungry flies. As I lifted my head in sudden fear, thunder rolled across the sky, and lightning flared in horizontal shafts, showing a thick bank of iron-gray clouds in the sky I couldn't otherwise see.

Just what I needed, a thunder and lightning storm.

As I had the thought, I remembered the storm at Farmer Blue's place. A sense of bittersweet nostalgia swept through me. I'd thought I was miserable then.

My current situation illustrated how wonderful my life had been.

I'd been home. I'd had a job. And I'd had all my friends.

Even if those derfs *had* left me to do that job alone.

I sighed, dropping wearily onto my back on the sandy soil.

The scent of ozone swept past on a moist breeze. I should try to find shelter.

It was frustrating not to be able to see where I was going. I could be standing right next to a house and have no idea.

Sighing again, fully immersed in my self-pity party, I shoved to my knees and then to my feet, reaching up to adjust Slimy on my shoulder.

He made an "mmpff" sound and shifted slightly, going back to sleep. I was pretty sure I'd heard a soft, croaking snore a few minutes back.

The thought made me smile. At least Slimy was getting some sleep.

I started forward again, almost immediately slamming my toes against a rock. "Arrrghhh!" I screamed, my hand flying up and energy dancing in my palm before I even realized what I'd done.

Well, der! I had a built-in flashlight under my skin. With a relieved smile, I sent energy into my hand and built the silvery power until it illuminated the space around me.

Then I refocused my attention ahead, planning to get my bearings and start off again.

And found myself looking at a creature with enormous pale blue eyes, spidery fingers that clutched the air in front of it, and enormous feet and ears.

I screamed.

And threw myself at him. "Hobs! I didn't think I'd ever see you again. How'd you find me?"

"We followed your magic," the hobgoblin told me, squeezing me back in a hug even harder than I was squeezing him. "I'm so happy to see you, Miss."

His words sifted through my ecstatic brain. *We... he'd said we!*

"Meow." A soft, warm body hit my ankles and my bones vibrated under a ferocious purr.

"Wicked!" I screamed, grabbing him up and burying my face in his fur. He smelled like sunlight and dust and home.

Claws scrabbled at my shirt, and I realized my movement had dislodged the frog. "Man going down! Man going down!" Slimy screamed.

Wicked reached over and planted a paw on the

frog, holding him against my shoulder before he could slip away.

"Ouch, watch those claws, feline...mmmfff!"

I giggled as Wicked licked the frog right on the lips. And then grimaced. "You're going to get boils or warts or something, Mr. Wicked."

The frog looked outraged, his voice filled with disgust. "How many times do we need to have this conversation? That's all fairy tale stuff. Frogs don't give people warts or any other disgusting skin conditions."

Wicked's tail snapped the air and he fixed me with a glowing orange gaze that provided enough light to clearly see the frog's disgust.

In fact, I realized, since my energy had fallen away in my excitement to see them, he'd been illuminating the area all by himself. The sigil on his chest was also glowing, and the combination of the two was giving off a pretty good light.

Wicked and his littermates had been bred to be powerful witch familiars. They each had a potent magical sigil to call, and Wicked's was a soul star sigil, a silver star inside a circle that was smaller than the points of the star. The sigils had been meant for use in dark, oily magic, but they worked just as well to amplify good magic and had been useful more than once when my friends and I had been up against a force that was too powerful for us to handle alone.

"You called your sigil without a circle or spell?"

"This place is not magic," Hobs told me. Apropos of what, I didn't know.

"I know, Walt told me..." My voice faded away as I remembered Walt was in danger.

"Who is Walt?" Hobs asked, cocking his over-sized head.

"A friend. And we need to help him. Demons have him."

Hobs looked worried. "Miss, the void is closing. If we don't leave this place soon, we'll have to stay here."

Despair filled my chest. "Do you know how to get out of here?"

Hobs frowned. "This place isn't magic..."

Impatience strummed against my last nerve. "I know that, Hobs. What does that have to do with anything?"

"...but it works as a magic mirror," the hobgoblin went on as if I hadn't interrupted. "It reflects magic back and makes it stronger."

I thought about what he'd said and realized I understood. "My keeper magics put a demon on her boohind and knocked her clean out."

Hobs nodded. "Yes. But you need to be careful, the mirror image of your magic is more powerful, but it's also unpredictable."

He was right. My keeper magics usually drew things to me. But in Plex, it had flung something away. There could be other surprises. "I'll keep that in mind. But why are you mentioning this?"

Hobs opened his mouth and then hesitated, closing it again. He held up a finger and then... disappeared. He reappeared a blink later with a goat in his arms.

My mouth fell open. "Is that...?"

Hobs said, "Ahhhhhhhhh!"

And the goat fell over, legs straight out from her body and bobbing slightly on the air.

"Adelaide? Where'd you find her?"

"She was just inside the breach when we came through. I took her back."

"You took her back?"

Hobbs nodded, folding his hands in front of him as the goat meandered away, nibbling on the unfriendly looking scruff embedded in the sandy dirt.

I stared at him for a long moment, thinking about everyone mentioning Hobs when we spoke about the wrinkle. Then it hit me. "You can dimension skip." Hobgoblins can pop into a different dimension when they're threatened and hiding or just because they want to. Generally, they don't have the power to carry much with them when they skip, but... "The mirroring magic let you carry her through the breach?"

He nodded.

"Bessy?" I asked, wondering if he'd found the cow too.

"She's home. Along with two other cows. We were looking for her when you came through or I could have taken you back too. By the time Wicked and I came back through, you were gone."

Blithering bat booty! If only Slimy and I had stuck around the breach... "Okay, great. Then take yourselves and Adelaide home. Slimy too. I need to find Walt."

"Not going to happen, Miss."

I looked at the hobgoblin, shocked by his refusal to listen to me. I'd told him he was a free man when he'd come to live at Croakies, but he usually listened to me anyway.

I just realized I didn't like it when he acted like a free man. What did that say about me?

Bad Naida, ugly Naida!

"It's not safe here, Hobs."

Pain slashed across my ankle. I jumped away from Wicked's claws and glared down at him. "Ow!"

"Yeow!" he yelled, clearly not on board with my suggestion that they leave.

"There's no reason for all of us to be stranded here. If Hobs can jump back and forth, he can come back and get me later."

Hobs shook his head. "The fold in the dimensions has altered the landscape. There will be no way to know where you are once it's severed."

Despair filled my chest. I would be stuck in Plex forever. I'd have to get used to thick, silver water, weird trees, entire families that looked like clones of each other, and weird Seers whose living rooms look like mountains.

But...Walt.

I sighed. "I can't leave without helping my friend, Hobs."

His huge blue eyes softened. "I know, Miss. And we're going to help too."

Realizing we were wasting valuable time arguing, I sighed, beaten. "Okay. But I'm not sure what I'm going to do for a living in a world without magic."

Wicked's tail snapped on the air. He made a grumbling noise that sounded like censure, though I had no idea what I'd done to annoy him that time.

"Let's go. Walt's been with them too long already. I'm really worried that we're going to be too late."

Watching my cat stalk away, Hobbs nodded. "Do you know where he is?"

"Erm...mmfff." I started off after Wicked, counting on his impeccable instincts to save me from monumental embarrassment. After the battle I'd put up trying to get them to leave me to do the job all by myself, I was determined not to let them know how truly useless I was in the search.

Hobs fell into step beside me. "Try looking with

your keeper magics," he told me, proving he hadn't been fooled by my non-answer to his question.

I thought about his suggestion, but I had no idea how to search for a non-artifact with my energy. Still, he'd been right about Plex's effect on magic. Maybe it would work.

I stopped, closed my eyes, and thought about tugging my energy forward. It nestled inside me, safe and happy in the spot deep at my core where I stored it. At first, the energy resisted my call. I wasn't surprised by that since I could give it no magical direction for an artifact. But I pictured Walt and it slowly unwound, streaming toward my fingertips on silvery threads. Energy erupted from my fingers, sending a burst of deadly power into the ground in front of Hobs and me. Dirt and rock flew into the air and ahead of us. My cat yowled his displeasure.

"Sorry, little man," I yelled.

I shared a look with Hobs, energy spreading over my hand and halfway up my arm. I glowed like a torch in a dark cave. "Oops," I said softly.

Hobs chuckled. "Mirror magic."

I took a deep breath and lifted my arm, sending the energy straight up into the sky so it could pick its own direction. The silvery energy shot skyward like a rocket, burst through the thick blanket of darkness like fireworks, and whirled away in sizzling streams that whistled shrilly as they cut through the murky dark.

I waited, listening for the telltale clang that proclaimed the discovery of an artifact...in this case Walt.

The first clang sounded in the distance. I turned to my right. "I think we might be going the wrong wa..."

Clang.

Clang.

Clang.

Clang.

My gaze followed the sounding of each discovery chime, my pulse shooting skyward as they built. There definitely weren't six Walts so...

Clang.

Clang.

Clang.

I frowned. "I don't think the magic is working," I told Hobs.

His head had been on a swivel, following the direction of each chime. "What's *that*, Miss?" he asked.

Something glowed with dull amber light in the distance. I narrowed my gaze at the object as it flew closer, the whisper of its passage through the air almost too soft to hear.

I realized too late that the object wasn't slowing down. It slammed into me a few seconds later and fell to my feet, smoking as if it had just come through the atmosphere.

"Ouch," I murmured, rubbing my shoulder where it had hit. "What is that?"

Hobs and I bent over it, but it was Slimy who identified the object first.

"A wand."

I narrowed my gaze at what looked like a simple stick. But I could see the glow of its tip beneath the soil. "A wand? What the..."

Another object soughed through the air and smacked into me, hitting me in the solar plexus and doubling me over in pain. I struggled to pull air into my lungs, wheezing loudly.

"Meow?" Wicked asked, sitting on my feet as I finally pulled air noisily into my chest.

"What in the world?" I wheezed.

Hobs picked it up and held it in front of his face. He pressed a button and vacuum sounds emerged. He giggled. "A hand vacuum, like the one Miss Lea has behind her counter."

"A vacuum," I said, rubbing my stomach. "What in the world would I do with that?" All I could think of was the rogue vacuum artifact at Croakies. It liked to eat books and shoes and people if I wasn't careful.

A sound like several arrows passing through air brought my head whipping up. I yelped in fear, "Incoming!" Crouching low, I covered my head, pulling Wicked into the protective curl of my body.

Hobs jumped away from us, and the whirring sound stopped a beat later. Silence reigned.

I risked an upward glance, finding several items, including a witch's athame and a deadly looking sword, hovering on the air around me.

Realization hit. *Wicked.* His presence had honed and focused my rogue magics and made them bow to his will. I kissed him on top of his soft head. "Good kitty."

He whacked me on the cheek with a paw, claws mostly sheathed, and sauntered out of my clutches, tail whipping.

The artifacts all slammed to the ground in a perfect circle around us. I looked at them, finding a large, burlap bag and a woman's purse in addition to the two blades. "Who would have guessed there'd be so many artifacts in a non-magic dimension?"

I sighed. "There's nothing here that will be any help finding Walt though."

Hobs bent down and smoothed his spidery fingers through the sandy dirt, uncovering something I hadn't noticed. When he picked it up, I thought it was a sundial, but as he handed it to me, I saw that the four directions were depicted on the surface of the dial. It was a compass.

I smoothed a finger over it, brushing sand away to find the four seasons depicted inside the directional symbols and the four elements inside that. It must have belonged to an Earth witch.

I pricked my finger on something on the face and blood smeared its surface before I could pull it away.

"Ouch!" I lowered the artifact. "Okay, I'll admit, I have no idea how to read this. I'm lost."

The compass vibrated in my hand, a bloody aura rising from its surface. I looked down at it and peered through the strange, red light, seeing the triangular blade in the center start to rotate. "Hey, this is doing something. The gnomon is moving."

Hobs moved closer. "It's blood magic, Miss."

I didn't like it. But however innocently I'd done it, I'd engaged the dial with a drop of my blood. Then, I realized there was probably a tiny blade somewhere on the surface of the thing for just that purpose. If we ever made it back home, I'd show it to Lea and get her opinion about the thing.

The gnomon stopped halfway between North and West, hovering on the line between earth and air. "I wonder what it's pointing to?"

"Meow!"

Wicked was heading into the night, a glow surrounding him as he walked in the same direction the compass was pointing.

Either he knew something I didn't...not an unusual occurrence if it was true...or he'd decided to trust the dial to help us find Walt.

Or...there was always that third option...Wicked had no idea where he was going, and I'd just be going along for the ride.

12

BETWEEN YOUR HOPES AND EXPECTATIONS...

*T*he ground rose slowly as we walked. So slowly, in fact, I didn't notice it until my calves started to ache and I was panting as I breathed. Wicked was well ahead of me, Hobs had shot away a while back and I hadn't seen him since. I was pretty sure he was just doing the Road Runner thing, tearing around leaving a visible cartoon trail behind him, and was hoping he wouldn't decide I was Wile E. Coyote in training.

I was carrying the artifacts I'd drawn with my keeper magics inside the burlap sack that had come with them. If the bag was an artifact as I had to assume it was, I had no idea what purpose it served. But it did come in handy for carrying the other artifacts, since I didn't feel I could leave them lying around after I'd enticed them to one spot.

I jolted to a sudden stop with a yelp as a wall

loomed up in front of me. It took me a moment to figure out that I was looking at an enormous ridge which appeared to rise straight up into the sky, nearly as far as I could see.

From somewhere high above my head, I heard the hobgoblin cackling and my cat giving an answering yowl. The moist night seemed to swallow up Wicked's meow. If I hadn't already figured out where they were, the rock that tumbled down the ridge and hit me between the eyes would have been a pretty good clue.

I should have never let them run ahead without me. "Hey, you two!" I whisper-yelled. "Get down here right now before you kill yourselves."

A hearty breeze flared up, sending my long brown hair swirling into my face and blinding me. As the breeze died down, a butcher shop stench sifted past, and I grimaced under its power. "Ugh! You guys, come here." A stout sense of foreboding fueled my whisper, turning it into a louder-than-I'd-intended whisper-shout.

Flames shot out of an opening in the rocky wall. I shifted the burlap sack, grabbing hold of Slimy as I leaned back to look up. The terrible twosome was halfway up the wall, standing on a path that wound along the rocky face and looked too narrow to support anything bigger than a hobgoblin or a cat.

I certainly wasn't going to try to cart my wide boohind up that path.

Rain bounced off my upturned nose and splashed into my eyes. I closed my eyes and rubbed them hard, the water stinging like sand in my tender baby blues.

"Yeow!" Wicked told me with the kind of snotty tone that only a cat can achieve.

I looked up again, prepared to yell at them for not coming down. Were they higher than the last time I'd looked up? *Dribbling dragon slobber!*

"Come down here, you two."

Rain arrived with a deep-throated rumble, lightning flaring sideways across the leaden sky as it had before, and the stinging drops drove me to seek cover. Thunder vibrated in my teeth as I pressed closer to the wall in a fruitless attempt to escape the deluge.

A blood-curdling scream sliced through the rain and thunder. My gaze shot upward, and I clocked the back of my head against the wall as I took in the fire blasting from the opening near the top of the ridge.

"Walt!" I breathed out in horror, rubbing my head. What were they doing to him?

There was a soft thump, and a furred form hit the ground. I glanced over at Adelaide, who'd clearly fainted from the scream. I'd forgotten about the little goat. "Sorry, girl," I whispered.

Another jolt of lightning illuminated the cat and the hobgoblin above. They'd nearly reached the opening. I wanted to scream at them to stop, but I knew they wouldn't listen even if they could hear me over the thunder and rain.

Draping the handles of the sack across my torso, I carefully placed Slimy inside so he'd be safe and my hands would be free.

It would be a miracle if I survived the climb along that narrow winding path, in the dark, over a rain-slick surface.

A miracle.

"You're right, you shouldn't try it," Slimy agreed to my unspoken thought. "You're very wide and the path is pretty narrow."

I stuck my tongue out at the bag.

"I saw that," the frog said.

"You did not." I looked at the path, sighing. The frog was right. I was so much wider than that track. But having no other choice, I found the bottom of the footpath and started climbing.

Five feet up the path, I slipped and nearly plunged back to the ground. Digging my fingertips into the craggy rock face, I managed to keep from falling. But I tore some painful gashes in the tips of my fingers in the process. I took a deep breath and started climbing again, moving more slowly.

My butt took a hit and I shrieked, flailing my arms in an attempt to keep from falling. It was no use. I tumbled the six feet I'd managed to travel, landing on my feet with a colorful word on my lips.

I looked up into the sweet face of the goat.

"Ahhhhhhhhhh!" she screamed.

I shushed her. "You're going to bring the demon hordes down on our heads."

She blinked at me, her jaw making the usual chewing motions. Then she started up the path on nimble hooves, apparently forgetting about me altogether.

I sighed and started up again.

A sizzling sound from above preceded another rush of flame from the cave opening. I listened in dread for another scream, but there was only silence. That was a very good thing because the cat and Hobs were no longer climbing the wall. I had to assume they'd gone inside.

I tried to climb faster, nearly falling two more times before I bumped up against the goat and couldn't go any further.

Adelaide stood happily on the narrow path, nibbling leaves off a scrubby tree that clung to the rocky face. "Move, goat! I need to get up there."

She ignored me, plucking another leaf from the little tree.

Rain pelted us from above. The occasional flash of lightning only served to highlight the ferocity of the storm around us, and a blustery breeze had kicked up to turn my wet skin to ice. My teeth were clacking together as I huddled as close to the rock as

I could get. A particularly violent shiver nearly toppled me off the path.

I contemplated trying to step over the goat, but decided that way lay suicide. All she would need to do was start moving while I had a leg over her back and I'd be toast.

"Adelaide, you need to move." I couldn't shake the thought that a loud noise would mean her death too. If she fainted on that narrow path, there'd be only one way to go. Down. Far down.

I patted her boohind and she finally got the idea, breaking off another leaf before turning and heading up the path again.

As we neared the cave opening, the horrible stench I'd smelled before grew until my eyes watered from it. The scent was familiar, but I couldn't quite place where I'd smelled it before. It smelled like a combination of rotting fish, dirty socks and biological substances.

The path ended just below the opening. It was two feet beneath the cave, and I'd need to step up to get inside. The goat stopped a foot away and went to work plucking leaves off another scrub tree.

I leaned against the wet, slippery surface to listen, hearing nothing inside.

After a moment, Adelaide turned and hopped the space between the path and the cave, disappearing inside just before another plume of fire sprayed the entrance.

"Adelaide!" I screamed before I could stop myself. I jumped into the cave, rolling away from the edge and keeping a low profile in case fire filled the opening again.

I didn't even realize I'd drawn the wand until I looked at my hand and saw it there. The tip glowed with pinkish light, sending spots of illumination dancing over the walls. I shoved to my feet, prepared to do battle with the demons to save my friends.

But I was destined to be disappointed in that.

The cave was empty except for Adelaide, who was snorfling along the wall as if searching for more leaves.

What in the…?

"Ahhhhhhhhhh!"

Flames shot out from a shadowed corner in the back and I dove to the ground, sliding across the rocky floor on my belly. The flames illuminated the cave and I saw a huge form huddled against the wall. The thing had a long, elegant head, small ears, and a large, spiked body that tapered to a long tail. The tail was curled around the body and a pale face with wide, terrified eyes was folded inside the appendage, trapped within the spikes.

A dragon! No wonder I'd remembered that scent. I'd stumbled into a dragon's nest one other time, and it was hard to forget the experience.

As the flame died down, the dragon and its prisoner disappeared too.

"Meow!"

A soft head bumped against me. "Wicked. You're okay. Thank the goddess."

"Miss? The magic here is strong."

I climbed to my feet, adjusting the bag over my shoulder.

A muffled voice came to me from its depths. "Let me out of here. You nearly killed me with that last move. Crazy lady."

Slimy! I'd forgotten about him when I'd flung myself to the floor. I quickly dug him out, holding him in front of my face. "I'm sorry. If I hadn't jumped, you and I would have both been Dragon BBQ."

He made a sound of disgust. "Don't ever talk about being cooked to a frog."

I looked around, the wand still clutched in my hand. As I'd seen before, the cave was empty. So, why had I seen Walt and the dragon when the flames had come? And where had Hobs and Wicked been?

"They're behind a magic wall," Hobs told me. "We were trying to talk to it, but the dragon doesn't seem to understand us. I think it's trapped in its feral form."

I knew a couple of dragons. Even considered one of them a friend, and I could imagine how Birte would feel if she was trapped as a dragon. "Maybe we can help."

Hobs frowned. "I think it's this place, Miss."

"Because it amplifies magic?"

He nodded. "The dragon is its magical form, so that's the form the dimension forces her to stay in. She can't escape it."

"How'd she get hold of Walt?"

"As far as I can tell from your friend's mumblings, she snatched him from the demon."

"I need to get through that wall." I looked down at the wand. Hmmm, I wonder. I held it up, "Bibbity Bobbity Boo!"

Nothing happened.

"Maybe you need to think about what you want it to do," Slimy said.

I took a deep breath, pointed the wand at a spot in the center of the wall, and thought about the wall disintegrating. The wand vibrated in my hand. Hope flared. The pink tip glowed almost red, bulged outward, and spit a rainbow of flowers into the air.

I groaned, watching the flowers drift harmlessly to the ground. "It must have belonged to a witch with a passion for gardening." I shoved the wand back into the burlap bag.

Hobs held out his hand. "I'll take you inside, Miss."

I settled Mr. Slimy on the ground next to Wicked. "Take care of each other," I told them.

"Ahhhhhhhhhhh!" Adelaide screamed, spitting out bits of the silvery leaves she'd been chewing.

All of the blood drained from my face as the center of the wall started to glow and grew semi-transparent. I could see the dragon's jewel-colored, slanted eyes through the illumination and realized what was about to happen.

Adelaide looked too much like food to the feral creature. If she stayed where she was, she was going to be dragon kibble in about two seconds.

But, as the illumination grew and the flame behind the wall coalesced into something deadly inside the dragon's open maw, I realized I'd never make it to the goat in time.

There was only one thing to do. I opened my mouth and shrieked loud enough to wake the dead. Or make a fainting goat faint.

Thump. Adelaide hit the ground.

The lethal flames roared harmlessly over her prone form, out into the still-rainy night. I raised the sword I hadn't realized I'd grabbed, and leaped toward the opening created by the dragon's fire-magic.

13

ABOVE THE FEAR OF THEIR LOSS...

I landed on the edge of a foot-high rim of sticks and rocks, stumbling forward and barely catching myself before I fell into the slimy, stinky debris covering the bottom of the nest. The dragon threw back her head and roared, sending a fresh stream of fire in my direction. I dove to the side, heat searing the hairs on my arm but not quite burning me.

The dragon surged to her feet, tail unwinding and lashing out so quickly I barely had time to jump the muscular appendage before I was skewered.

"Run, Walt!" I yelled as the unfurling tail left him free. He didn't waste any time. With an agile leap from the nest, Walt hit the shimmering magic of the wall and tumbled through, rolling to his feet on the other side.

I was right behind him.

The dragon burst through a beat later, her gaze like a forest fire in a windstorm, wild and raging as she opened her mouth again.

I thought about the contents of my artifact bag. Was there anything I could use?

Fiery death shot in my direction. On pure instinct, I lifted the sword in front of Walt and me, expecting to be burned alive.

But the fire hit the blade and spun backward, returning to the dragon and sizzling harmlessly over her opaline scales.

She tried two more times with the same result, and then slid her deadly tail over the floor of the cave, the agile appendage skimming dangerously close to Mr. Wicked and friends.

"Get out of here!" I yelled to them. But before they could move toward the door, the dragon was suddenly there, blocking the opening with her huge, enraged form.

To my surprise, she didn't fling fire at us or try to skewer us with her tail. I looked into her eyes and saw something there that broke my heart. She looked...sad.

I turned to Walt. "Why are you here?"

He was pale and panting, but his gaze was on the dragon's too and I could tell her sadness was affecting him. "She took me from the demons and brought me here."

"She didn't try to eat you?" Slimy asked, hopping closer.

Walt fixed a startled look on the frog and shook his head. "No. I think she's just lonely."

"Hobs says she's locked into her dragon form," I said. "If there are no other dragons in Plex, that means she's alone. And will be for the foreseeable future."

"We could take her home with us," Hobs said, his blue gaze liquid with compassion.

It was an idiotic idea. An impossible one.

Which, of course, was why I agreed to do it.

D awn was breaking over the horizon by the time we'd talked the dragon into coming with us and started off again. After much discussion, we decided that Hobs would stay on the ground because he could move fast. He'd carry Slimy, mostly because the frog refused to get back into the burlap sack, insisting it smelled like dirty feet in there. I had Wicked clutched in my arms, and Adelaide was lying across Walt's legs. He grinned down at her as she let us know in her unfailing way that she was unhappy with her seat high in the sky.

Sure, he thought it was funny now. He probably wouldn't think all the caterwauling was funny after a couple of hours.

We rode between the spikes of the dragon's long, elegant back, the sun a warm promise on our faces as we headed toward the border we'd been trying to reach before we were attacked by demons.

That seemed like days ago.

I had to admit, it was pretty cool riding a dragon. When I got home, I was going to convince Birte to give me the occasional ride around Enchanted just for giggles.

Home. The thought made me both happy and sad. I wasn't at all convinced we were ever going to see Enchanted again. There was a really good chance we'd be too late to make it across the breach. "Tell me what you have in mind once we get there," I yelled over the wind.

Walt half-turned my way, his expression relaxed. "I'm going to try to convince the Seer at the border to open the gate."

I frowned. "Won't the wrinkle keep us from getting into the right dimension?"

"It doesn't work that way. A border gate is like one of those spinning doors. You select your destination by thought and intention."

"Wait, if there's a gate, why don't we just use it to leave? Why do we need a Seer at all?"

"It's not that easy. The gate is hidden unless a Seer calls it forward. And the PTB have declared that no one is to leave Plex because of something that's been going on in the Universe."

I was pretty sure I knew what that something was. Things had been wonky for a while. My friends who'd been around long enough to have direct knowledge of the first *Dark Rages* were speculating that we might have another one if the magic wasn't untangled soon. They thought somebody was behind the problems with the PTB process. I suddenly wondered if it could be a Seer. "Do you think this Seer will help us?"

Walt shrugged. "That depends upon who I'm talking to. Some of the Seers are risk-averse."

"Do you know the Seer we're going to talk to?"

He shook his head. "No. The only Seer I've ever met is the one in Wilshire Plex. He's been there for centuries so he wouldn't have any knowledge of border issues."

I thought of the advice we'd gotten from the Seer with the antique watch in his pocket. "Even if he did, we probably wouldn't understand it."

Walt nodded and fell silent.

I didn't instigate any further conversation. Mainly because my mind was swirling with questions and possibilities. The lockdown on Plex fit well into the recent problems with PTBs and the artifact process I'd been experiencing. Was it another piece in the puzzle Madeline Quilleran was trying to solve? And, if so, how did it fit? What were the Seers doing when they left Plex? Were they deliberately setting about to entangle the magical processes? Or was the discombobulation simply the result of their breaking magical law?

I promised myself I'd talk it over with Madeline when...if...I got back. Maybe we could find the missing Seers and turn them over to the Universe. If they were captured, maybe things would go back to normal in my world.

Or maybe there *was* no normal there. A part of me believed that chaos was the normal course of business at Croakies. And I honestly couldn't imagine it being any other way.

At some point in my musings, I must have fallen asleep. I jolted awake when my seat fell out from under me, and gave a sharp scream as the dragon leaned to the left and set her wings against the air in a braking motion.

Wicked yowled as I squeezed him close, but didn't smack me with a claw to gain release. Even the fearless feline apparently wasn't keen on falling a mile out of the sky to splat against the rocky dirt of Plex.

T he reality of the Plex border was decidedly underwhelming. It consisted of a small hut in the middle of a wide-open, vegetation-free zone that was scoured by wind and baked by the dual suns. A small creature in an oversized, hooded white robe stood outside the hut, arms crossed over its middle and hands tucked beneath the robe. The face which was mostly covered by the hood, pointed skyward, watching the dragon descend with no visible sense of surprise.

Most likely, living in a neutral zone between several dimensions, most of them magical, would make a person immune to such things. Though I didn't know how a person could ever become used to seeing a dragon in full flight. Especially one with a goat, a cat, and two people perched on its back.

The dragon made a surprisingly gentle landing, and I breathed a sigh of relief. Then it hopped ten feet off the ground before stopping, and the hop caught us completely off guard.

I flew off of the dragon's back and somersaulted through the air with Wicked caterwauling in my arms. I was vaguely aware of Walt flying past, still holding Adelaide, and heard the thump-slide-splat of their landing right after mine.

We lay there groaning for a beat. I didn't know about Walt, but I was busy cataloging my potential injuries before I tried to stand.

Everything seemed to be in working order, so I shoved upright, groaning loudly. Nothing was broken, but that didn't mean everything wasn't bruised and painful.

Wicked scampered toward the hut as a small

figure dressed in a white tunic, white pants, and a red and green Christmas scarf stepped out of it.

Blast the goddess's green panties! Hobs had beat us there. Next time I was riding the hobgoblin instead of the dragon. It would be faster and far less...fall-y.

A tiny green form hopped to greet Wicked, earning a touch to his nose as they met up. I smiled as I always did when I saw the frog and cat together. They were such an odd match-up. And so adorably weird.

The dragon's long body rippled, the wings snapping against the air, and it coughed out a cloud of gray smoke.

As the Seer approached, the dragon stepped backward, moving to stand behind Walt and me as if we were going to protect her.

I rolled my eyes, a wave of nostalgia for Sebille hitting me as I did. She performed the disgusted eye-roll so much better than me. I spoke over my shoulder to the massive reptile whose very deadly snout was mere inches from the back of my neck. I knew this because I could feel her "just this side of painful" hot breath on my skin. "You know he can still see you, right?"

The dragon huffed out another cloud of smoke, making Walt and I cough.

"Welcome," said a light, feminine voice.

I blinked in surprise, barely refraining from glancing toward Walt. The Seer was a woman. I gave her a smile, my fingers twitching to offer her a hand-shake before I caught myself. Walt hadn't welcomed my attempt to shake hands before, so I assumed Plexians didn't do it. Not every dimension saw the common Earthly greeting practice as harmless and friendly. Some apparently drew weapons when a hand was offered without being encouraged. "Hello. I'm Naida, Keeper of the Artifacts in the Earth dimension."

Walt gave the woman a low bow. Very low. Comically low. His nose touched his knees before he straightened again. He looked at me and despair razored through me. There was no way I could touch my knees with my nose. I'm not bendy like that.

"Um..." I said. "Okay, well..." I bent as well as I could and was happy when my eyes got close enough to see my knees.

Go me.

The Seer pushed back the hood, revealing shiny red hair, moss-green eyes, a pretty freckled face, and a smile that told me she'd noted my embarrassing lack of bendiness. Fortunately, she seemed willing to give me the unbendy-Earth-woman pass. "I am Diandra. It will be my pleasure to serve. How might I aid you in your journey?"

My journey? Apparently, old Diandra wasn't going to invite us to stay. She seemed anxious for us to be on our way. Lucky for her, I shared that sentiment. "We were accidentally pulled into Plex by a dimensional wrinkle. We wish to return to our own dimension."

Diandra stared at me a long moment, her pert nose wrinkling slightly, which made her more approachable and less Seer-like. "My heart breaks to disappoint. I'm sure Wilshire Walt has informed you of the impossible nature of your request."

I snorted and both Plexians looked at me as if I had frog poop on my face. Wait? Did I have frog poop on my face? I ran a hand over my nose and cheeks, finding nothing and gave them a thoughtful expression. "Yes, erm, Wilshire..." I couldn't finish. The moniker made my buddy Walt sound like a gunslinger in a really bad Western movie. "Walt explained to me that the gate has been closed."

Diandra shook her head. "It is worse than that. I'm afraid someone has sheered the wrinkle off. The original path you took is no longer viable. I'm afraid you are stranded here in Plex." She tried a smile, possibly hoping to soften the bad news. "I'm sure you will enjoy living here. We are a very likable people."

A range of emotions slid over my face. Horror, anger, fear, more horror... I suddenly found it hard to breathe and I struggled not to melt into a puddle of despair.

Misreading my emotional turmoil, Diandra took a step back and lifted her hands, pale green energy flaring from her palms.

The sight made my stomach twist with distress. Between the red hair and freckles, and the earth-tinged magic, Diandra reminded me too much of Sebille. I missed Sebille. I missed Lea. I even missed Madeline Quilleran. In that moment they seemed even farther away than they had since I'd first become stranded in Plex.

"I'm sorry, Miss," Hobs said. "I tried to pop home, but I ended up in a different dimension. I can't get us back anymore."

Tears burned in my eyes. I sniffed, nodding. "Okay, well..."

"Where is the nearest Artifact Keeper?" Walt asked, surprising me.

Diandra blinked in surprise, her expression thoughtful. "Keeper? Let's see, I believe Dimension thirteen has one. The Lang Dimension. But the Keeper resides on the far side of the dimension. It's quite a trek. Also, there's a Universal Depot on twenty-four. It would be possible to reach a Keeper using the depot."

Hope flared. I turned to Walt and gave him a wide smile. "You're a genius."

His smile settled my roiling stomach. "Do you think it will work?" he asked.

Having traveled from one dimension to another using a depot once before, I knew it would work, but I wasn't looking forward to the experience. And I wasn't entirely sure I had the firepower to use a depot by myself. When I'd gone before, Wicked and I had been guided by Madeline Quilleran. Without the witch...

I gave Diandra an assessing look. Her green eyes widened and she did a thing with her head where she adjusted it backward on her neck, like an ostrich. "Do you know how to engage a Universal Depot?"

She paled, no easy feat given the fact that she already had milk-white skin. "That is outside my purview as Seer..."

"Naida is a person of great importance to the Universe," Walt said quickly.

Diandra hesitated, giving me an assessing look. But she shook her head. "I...I am not at liberty..."

"Her loss would create stress in the system," Walt told the Seer. "It is your job as Seer to make sure that doesn't happen. I believe that makes aiding her safe transport out of Plex part of your job."

When Diandra continued to hesitate, I said, "Please? We only want to go home."

She eyed the burlap bag over my shoulder, a speculative gleam entering her gaze. "As I have said, it is outside my purview to aid you in leaving Plex."

Hope flew away on spindly wings. My shoulders sagged.

"However, I will consider a trade. My expertise for that bag."

I felt my eyes go wide. "This bag?" Sudden doubt replaced elation. "Why? What does it do?"

"You do not know?"

I shook my head, glancing at Walt. He shrugged.

She sighed. "It is a rare treasure. It produces what you need most in any given moment."

I thought of the sword that appeared in my hand in the dragon's lair. Embarrassment brought a flush to my face. If only I'd known.

The bag shifted against my hip and I looked down as Hobs reached a long-fingered hand into it and came away with a greasy bakery bag that smelled of chocolate. I blinked in surprise.

The Seer's pretty face brightened. "May I?" She reached toward the bag.

"Of course." I held it out to her and she placed a hand inside, pulling out a small book with a gilded title across its burgundy leather cover. She laughed in delight as she saw it. "I have been so dreadfully bored," she explained. "This hut isn't exactly entertainment central." She stared at the book as one might look at a cherished child.

I wanted in on the fun. Reaching into the bag, I felt something hard, smooth, and cylindrical in my hand. Excited, I pulled it out. And found myself looking at a bottle of shampoo. "What?"

Walt grimaced. "You do have a little dragon goo right..." He pointed to his head and I yelped, reaching up to find the strands of my hair glued together into a thick, sticky ribbon over one ear.

I glared at the stupid bag. "I've been disrespected by a magical artifact."

It was the story of my life.

Diandra giggled.

Reaching inside the bag, I pulled out the other artifacts. "I need to take these with me, but you can keep the bag. And this," I handed her the shampoo. "I have my own special blend at home." The thought that I might soon be home to use it made me smile despite having been dissed by the burlap bag.

Stupid magic artifact.

14

OH! LIP BALM!

I'd been dreading the journey to the depot. Really dreading it. After trekking across Plex, being attacked by magical creatures and the weather, I was ready to leap into the great, blue void and fall to Croakies for a shower and a bag full of tacos.

Unfortunately, all that would have to wait on logistics.

It was one thing to drop me, Wicked, Slimy, and Hobs into the void. But adding the goat and dragon definitely created a kink in the process.

At first, Diandra dug in her sandal-clad heels, insisting it couldn't be done and that Adelaide and the dragon, who's name I still did not know, would need to stay behind in Plex.

But I'd given the dragon my word that I'd take her with us, so she could have a chance at a normal life. And I'd told Farmer Blue I'd bring his goat home.

I was often a screwup. Sometimes I had no idea what I was doing. And I wasn't the most gifted artifact wrangler there ever was. But I had control over one thing in my life.

I could keep my word.

So I always tried to do that.

"You have to figure out a way," I told the stubborn Seer. "Meditate on it, if that helps. But the dragon and Adelaide need to come with us."

Diandra threw up her hands. "Then you can't use the depot," she insisted.

"Find us another way," I insisted more insistently. I added a meaningful glance at the bag for good measure.

Her face crumpled as she received the message I was sending. "I'll consult the flame tonight."

"Good," I said, nodding. Though I had no idea what that meant, specifically, I had a general idea it was something to do with throwing dust into a campfire. Pretty much everything a Seer did had something to do with that.

It was weird. But if it worked, I was in full support.

Later, as the two suns slipped down the horizon, I sat on a table-sized tree stump a few yards from the tiny hut and watched Diandra make her preparations.

Walt came out of the hut, letting the mud-covered wood door close softly behind him, and approached me with a small bowl of something I hoped included chocolate.

I wasn't disappointed. The treat he handed me consisted of vanilla ice cream on top of a frosted brownie. It was melting fast in the heat so I dug in quickly. "Mmmm," I closed my eyes in pleasure. "This is amazing."

Walt smiled. "The small one with long fingers took it from the bag." Walt frowned. "For one who is stranded far from home, his needs seem very simple and...unwavering."

I laughed. "Pretty much all chocolate all the time. I think I was a hobgoblin in a prior life."

Walt laughed, dropping onto the stump beside me.

"No, really," I told him, pulling my hair away from my ears. "See how far they stick out? And how they're kind of pointed on the top?"

Walt examined my ears carefully. "You do have blue eyes." He grinned, eyeing my empty bowl. "And an insatiable appetite for chocolate."

"Right?" I told him, grinning back.

We sat in companionable silence for a few minutes, watching Hobs and Wicked scamper around the dragon, playing hide and seek beneath her wings and tail.

Slimy sat on the ground in front of the enormous

reptile, his gaze locked on hers, and they seemed to be having a fairly extensive conversation.

Warmth blossomed in my chest at the sight. "I wish I knew her name."

Walt turned to me, surprise lighting his face. "The dragon? That's Kanish."

"Kanish? How'd you know?" Then I remembered he'd spent time with her in the cave.

"Once I heard her speak, I understood drago-nish, which is a mix of old Russian and an ancient Paleo-Indian dialect that originated in the Grand Teton mountains."

"Really?" I was fascinated despite myself. "Who knew?"

"Well, I did. And I presume other dragons knew as well."

Apparently, the rhetorical question wasn't a thing in Plex.

Sitting cross-legged in front of the fire, the Seer settled her robes around her legs and pulled a small bag from within the folds. "She's awfully young for a Seer."

"Don't be fooled by her looks. Plexians can't become Seers until they reach their one-thousandth year."

My eyes flared wide in shock. "A thousand?"

"She's probably nearer to fifteen hundred years old, I would guess." He frowned. "The Seers who left were close to three thousand years old. It is a massive loss of history and knowledge that Plex will never recover from."

"Do you think the missing Seers are the reason for the instability in the Universe?"

Walt gave that some real thought before answering. "It is possible. Probably even likely. The inner workings of the magical Universe depend heavily upon the proper use of the dimensional gate. Diandra tries her best, but with the others gone, things are getting missed. Accidental crossovers have tripled under her watch."

I nodded. "I've met some of the results."

"The demons," Walt nodded, grimacing. His gaze slid to the dragon and I knew he was thinking about her being trapped there. "Unfortunately, the accidents go both ways, as the loss of the Seers underscores."

"Could it be deliberate?" I asked Walt.

"What do you mean?"

"Could someone have been deliberately messing with the gate? Removing the Seers? Maybe even influencing dimensional magic to affect the Universe?"

Walt shrugged. "It seems unlikely. Universal magic is volatile at best. One would never know how a certain action might be interpreted within it."

"What do you know about the Dark Rages?" I asked my friend.

Walt shivered violently. I didn't know if it was

because of the falling nighttime temperatures or because of my question. "I wasn't alive during that time," he said. "But it hit Plex hard." He glanced my way. "The Rages started here, you know."

"I didn't know that. How did they begin?"

He opened his mouth to respond and then closed it, growing pale. "They started with a gate malfunction and a new Seer. Barnabus Caeruleum was only twelve hundred years old, I believe."

"He was the Seer?"

Walt nodded. "He accidentally opened the gate and it malfunctioned, locking open. A wizard and his magical spawn entered Plex and killed young Barnabus. The Wizard took over the operation of the gate and held it for almost a century, spewing evil across the dimensions, destroying the forces of good wherever he could find them. Enormous creatures clad in black iron uniforms stormed across the lands, thousands of them, slaughtering and impris-oning in the name of the Universe. You can imagine the result. Chaos, fear, and rage against magic and the Universe that it thrived on." Walt shook his head. "When the Universe finally understood the genesis of the problem, it cracked down hard on Plex. Plex-ians were forbidden to leave. The gate was locked down, only working during pre-determined times for specific reasons. Millions of our citizens were slaughtered by the warriors on both sides who flooded our dimension, spewing deadly magics across the land. Plex never recovered fully. Our water is no longer water in the sense that it once was. Much of our plant and animal life has died out and the ones who survived are changed in unfathomable ways. Plex was once a vibrant and powerful dimension, trusted by the Universe to control the best interests of all dimensions." He sighed. "We are a shadow of what we once were." Walt looked so sad, I wrapped an arm around his shoulders and hugged him close.

"What happened to the wizard? Was he captured?"

Walt frowned. "All we have are rumors. Some rumors say he escaped before Plex was locked down. Others say he slipped away in the night, hiding somewhere in Plex and escaping much later disguised as a creature with red eyes and a bad temper."

I thought of the Brahma bull and shuddered. That would explain a lot.

We sat quietly after that, thinking our separate thoughts, listening to the Seer's melodic chanting, and watching the light show from her flames and dust. Walt's description of the Dark Rages was horrifying.

I could see why the Universe had created the PTBs after that, to ensure it never happened again. But PTBs had been disappearing too. Or going rogue. And with the exact same scenario setting up that had caused the Rages before, I couldn't help wondering if someone wasn't manipulating events to send the magical world into chaos again.

But if that was the case, who would it be? Who stood to gain the most from an eruption of fear and violence across the multiple dimensions?

The Seer threw another handful of dust onto the fire and lifted her hands, placing them palms down above the flame. Her melodic voice filled the silence between Walt and me, and I relaxed as the sweet smoke from her meditation fire sifted toward us.

My eyes were closing, and I was at the edge of sleep when an explosion rocked the silence.

Beside me, Walt leaped to his feet and took off running.

My eyes shot open. I stood, my gaze sliding to the dragon and my little friends to make sure they were okay. A soft scream drew my attention to the fire, where Walt was throwing dust from the ground onto the Seer, whose robe was on fire.

She smacked at the flames in wild-eyed panic, fear turning her previously calm demeanor on its head. The dust wasn't helping.

I took off running toward the hut, diving through the mudded door and racing to the tiny kitchen. I grabbed the burlap bag and shoved my hand into it, praying it would work as proclaimed. My hand came out clutching a fire extinguisher. Running outside and screaming at Walt to stand back, I blasted the Seer with the extinguisher.

Diandra covered her face with her arms, still screaming as the foam doused the last of the fire from her robe. The heavy white cloth hung in tatters from her slender frame, showing a scorched cotton skirt and blackened calves beneath. "Are you badly burned?" I asked, flinging the extinguisher aside.

"I'm not sure." She staggered back and fell to her knees, crying out as her flesh hit the ground.

I looked at Walt, who just stood there, wringing his hands. "Help me get her inside." I'd ask the bag for some balm for the Seer's burns. And anything else I could think of.

At that moment, I'd give almost anything for Florence Nightingale's medical kit.

"Demons!" Hobs screamed.

The dragon surged to her feet, flipping around to roar a warning to the sky. The creature's long, spiked tail barely missed us as Walt and I half-carried the Seer toward the hut.

Just great! I thought crabbily. We didn't have enough to worry about already?

The dragon ran several steps and leaped into the air, roaring again as she pounded her wings and speared upward, flame shearing across the night sky.

"Lay her on the couch," I told Walt.

Beyond the thin walls of the tiny hut, I heard the

unmistakable cries of pain and fear that told me fighting had broken out.

"Goddess keep Kanish safe," I prayed quietly as I worked to pull the robes aside so I could assess the damage. Her legs had taken the worst of it. But her hands were also blackened and blistered from smacking the flames in an attempt to put them out. "I looked at Walt. "Get the bag."

He nodded and ran toward the kitchen.

The door opened behind me. I spoke without looking up. "Hobs, you need to get Slimy and Wicked and bring them in here. We're going to need to fortify this place somehow against the demons."

The Seer moaned in pain, her head thrashing violently. I placed a hand on her arm in an attempt to soothe. "It's going to be okay. We've got the bag."

Walt ran back into the living room and skidded to a stop, his eyes going wide. "Oh!"

I gave him an impatient glance. "Walt, the bag? Hurry, she's in pain."

There was a soft rustling of fabric, and someone knelt down beside me. "Burns?" asked a familiar voice.

My head snapped around. Joy filled me and I gave a squeal, wrapping my assistant in a desperate but joyful hug. "You found us!"

Sebille rolled her eyes. "Of course, I found you. I'm the daughter of the queen of the Fae."

I squealed again and hugged her tighter.

Sebille reared back, dislodging my arms. "Now that I'm deaf from having you screaming in my ear..." She placed a hand above the Seer's blistered calves, staring into the woman's eyes. "This will hurt."

Tears slipped down Diandra's face. "Thank you, Princess."

To my utter shock, Sebille didn't correct the woman. Instead, she glanced at me. "Go help the dragon. She's heading back, and she's got three demons on her tail."

I didn't ask Sebille how she knew that. Nor did I ask how I was going to help since I was...well...me. I ran out the door and found myself standing in the dusty yard holding the sword artifact in one hand and a woman's purse in the other. I frowned down at one and gripped the other tighter.

Narrowing my gaze on the purse, I dropped it in the dust. My keeper magics were wonky at best in Plex.

Sebille's voice sifted through the door. "Get the horns."

"Huh?"

Kanish roared a warning and lowered her wings, flattening out as she hit the ground and skidded, her enormous form leaving a wide, smooth trail in the dirt.

I didn't have time to see if she was badly hurt. The black shapes above my head were coming in fast, their evil gazes glowing malevolently through the night.

I lifted the sword and ran toward them.

The first demon landed at a dead run, heading right for me.

A small form flew out of the darkness, leaping onto the demon's shoulders and grabbing its horns in long, spindly fingers.

The demon screamed as if in great pain. Hobs wrenched the horns violently, driving the monster to its knees.

The second demon hit the ground and half ran, half flew at me. I was ready. Lifting the blade, which glowed silver against the darkness, I swung as hard as I could. A warm, hard weight landed on my feet as the blade cut the darkness in a wide, horizontal strike and severed the demon's horns from its wide head with a single slice.

The horrible creature screamed as if it was on fire and fell to the ground, thrashing wildly.

I'd started to turn when the third demon hit me, sending us both flying across the yard. We hit the dirt and all the air was knocked out of my lungs as the demon's weight crashed into me.

Deadly-looking teeth snapped mere inches from my throat. I shoved a hand under the monster's chin, my arm muscles straining to keep it away as my mind sifted through the available options.

My magic rose up in a terror-fueled wash and

sprayed out from my palm, unfocused and too scattered to do much but hack him off. But it did distract the demon for a moment as I fought to get free.

He roared, slapping a hand onto his face as my magic bit into his eyes. The glow died out of his terrifying gaze, and I knew I'd scored a hit.

I tried to pull more energy forward, but I was too stressed. All I could manage was another unfocused wash of weak energy. I slammed a knee upward into the demon's belly and he arched away from me, still rubbing his streaming eyes.

Shoving free of the demon's weight, I nearly managed my escape. But at the last moment, his big hand snaked out and grasped my ankle, the deadly claws digging painfully into my skin.

Screaming in pain and fear, I kicked out with my other leg, clipping him in the jaw and snapping his head back. But it wasn't enough to get him to release me.

My hand scrabbled against the ground, looking for a rock or something to hit him with. Or even better, the sword I'd dropped when he'd barreled into me.

My hand wrapped around something heavy and pliable. Looking at the purse in my hand, I wanted to scream my frustration. I pulled the bag close and, feeling ridiculous and inadequate, I pelted him in the head with the soft, cloth bag.

He grunted at the first strike. That was when I

realized how heavy the purse was. But not because it had been magically enhanced. It was chock full of stuff.

The demon yanked me back by my ankle, his claws ripping my skin.

I struggled, mewling in terror and desperate to get free. I did the only thing I could think to do. Reaching into the purse with a prayer that it was like the burlap sack, I thought of a weapon.

My hand closed over a smooth cylinder and I tugged it out, spraying it into the demon's still streaming red eyes.

The creature's head whipped back and it sneezed.

I looked at the canister and wanted to swear. Hairspray.

"Okay Universe, you can stop messin' with me any time now," I screamed. I tried again and my searching fingers came up with a hairbrush.

I threw it at him.

A compact. I threw that at him too. It bounced off his hard, black scales and hit the ground.

The demon opened its mouth and showed me curved, knife-like teeth. "Looks like you're outgunned," he said nastily.

I threw a wad of tissues aside. Used. Ugh! A scarf. Maybe I could strangle him with it? Nah. A small sewing kit. Hand lotion. Lip balm. Gum. A protein bar. I'd have to snack on that later if I lived. Pantyhose...seriously? A crossword puzzle book. Nasal spray. I squirted that at the demon. Nothing. Keys. I tried jabbing him with those but they couldn't penetrate the dense scales. A pad of paper. I searched for the pen. Maybe I could stick that in his eyes. A handful of coins. I flung those at his face. A wallet. Empty. *Figures.* The pen! I jabbed it toward the demon's face but he jerked back, smacking my hand so hard the pen went flying.

Dancing demon digits!

Saliva hit my arm, burning like acid against my skin. The demon lowered its head, teeth fully bared. He was going to bite me!

I dug more frantically. *Mace*! I sprayed him in the eyes and the monster reared back, shrieking.

Gotcha!

My hand closed over a pair of nail scissors. I yanked them out as I scrambled out from under him. I looked at the creature's horns and back at the scissors.

There was no chance they'd cut the two-inch-wide horns.

Then again, the tips were much skinnier.

Any cutting at all should distract him, right?

The demon started to rise, I had to move fast. I jumped onto his back and quickly snipped the tip off one horn.

He roared, tossing his head back and nearly flinging me off.

I tried to reach the second horn with the scissors, but he was flailing around too much. I was clutching him like a monkey clinging to its mother, shrieking with fear.

A clawed hand raked down my arm, slicing me open from elbow to wrist.

I was so soaked in adrenaline I barely felt it. Grabbing the horn with my bleeding hand, I tried to bring the other hand over to cut it with the scissors.

Blood slicked the surface, causing the scissors to slip out of my grip.

In sheer desperation, I gritted my teeth and yanked at my magic. It surged forward, filling my palm with dense silver light. I slammed my hand against the horn, sending a thick stream of burning energy right into the tip I'd cut.

The demon's head slammed up on a roar, clocking me hard on the chin. I went down. My head bounced off the hard-pack dirt, and the edges of the world grayed as my mind started to shut down.

My fingers found something in the dirt and wrapped around it as I fought the darkness, battling for consciousness.

Footsteps clomped closer. A face appeared above mine, judgmental green eyes assessing me. "Good idea," Sebille said, snatching the thing I'd been clutching out of my hand.

I lay there a moment, panting. When the wooziness finally cleared, I shoved upright, my head screaming.

I focused my gaze on Sebille just in time to see her zip tie the last demon, smacking him on the head with an energy-infused palm as he tried to rouse himself enough to fight her.

She tromped over and looked down at the mess of stuff in the dirt. "Oh, lip balm!"

15

THE EPICENTER OF A NIGHTMARISH DESPOTISM

"Who carries zip ties in their purse?" Sebille asked. "It's pure genius."

"It's an *endless stuff* artifact," I told her, smiling. I'd finally figured out why the purse was an artifact. No matter how many times I jammed my hand into the thing, new stuff always appeared to fill it. I finally stopped when I pulled a pair of men's boxers from the purse. Ew! "Now, spill it," I told the Sprite. "How'd you find us?"

She reached into her pocket and pulled out the Book of Pages. It expanded as it hit the air, becoming the full-sized book. "Maude did a temporary spell so it would cross dimensions. But we need to get back within twenty-four hours or the spell expires."

I frowned.

She frowned.

I lifted my brows.

She rolled her eyes. "What?"

"I can't leave yet. I have a culprit or an artifact to find."

Sebille slid a look toward the goat. "The cows are home with the Blues. There's the goat. You finished the job."

"No. I finished the job Farmer Blue hired me to do, but we still don't know why the wrinkle happened."

"A quirk of fate?"

I shook my head. "I think somebody's orchestrating another Dark Rages."

All the blood left her face, leaving behind a lot of pale skin and freckles. "That's a terrifying thought."

"It is, I know. It might all be my imagination, but I don't think it is." I filled her in on my conversation with Walt.

When I was finished, Sebille was frowning. "Okay, I'll admit that's concerning."

I nodded.

"Any idea how to find the culprit?"

I glanced at the mess from the purse. "Maybe there's a clue finder somewhere in all that clutter."

Sebille laughed. "I wouldn't discount that as a serious possibility. I mean, there's a Phillips-head screwdriver in that thing, and...is that a banana?"

"I already ate the pears."

The door slammed and we turned as Walt strode our way. "She's resting from the healing." He gave

Sebille a shy smile. "That was amazing, by the way. I've never seen someone healed before."

Sebille shrugged, but her face pinkened under his compliment. I eyed them as a horrible thought occurred.

They liked each other.

Chunky cherub chins! Leave it to Sebille to like a boy who lived in an impossible-to-reach dimension.

"Anywhooooo," I said, my eyebrows peaking. "Walt, we were just talking about the wrinkle. I think someone's trying to bring on another Dark Rages."

"And we have just twenty-four hours...well, probably closer to twenty-three hours now...to find the culprit," Sebille added. "Any ideas?"

"Actually," he flushed. "Diandra and I were talking about that too. She agrees. And she says she doesn't think the other Seers left on their own. In fact, she doesn't think they left at all."

"Why does she think that?" I asked.

"Apparently, Seers have some kind of connection to each other. Ancient bonding magic. And she says she can still feel the other Seers, all seven of them. But the link is weak and feels somehow muffled."

"Like maybe they're locked up somewhere?" Sebille asked.

"Or dead," I said, frowning. I'd worked with a bonding artifact once. It was presented as a large tube of glue, which, when used to literally bond two people together, created an unbreakable magic connection that stuck even after the glue stopped working on their skin. I'd seized it from a fellow sorcerer whose special magics included relationship enhancement and marriage counseling. Needless to say, using the sometimes-destructive artifact to bond two unsuspecting humans was against the rules of the Magical Universe. Thus my order to retrieve it.

Walt nodded. "Death *would* mute the connection but probably wouldn't sever it completely."

"But the fact that she still feels them probably means they're in Plex," Sebille added.

I nodded agreement. "It seems unlikely the connection would hold across dimensions."

I glanced around, looking for my little friends. "Where'd Hobs, Wicked, and Slimy get off to?"

"And the goat?" Walt added.

Sebille flapped her hand toward a distant rocky ridge. "Last I saw them, Hobs had loaded the demons onto the dragon's back and was instructing her to take them over there."

I glanced at Walt. "Do you know what's there?"

He nodded. "It used to be a temporary holding cave during the Rages. It's been spelled to hold all kinds of magical creatures." He frowned. "I have no idea if the spell is still working."

I hoped Hobs knew what he was doing. But if it all fell apart, I was sure that, between the dragon and the screaming goat, we'd have some warning.

"I'll go check on them in a minute," I said,

glancing at Walt. "I'd like to set a trap for whoever is manipulating the dimensional borders. Do you have any suggestions?"

He thought about it for a moment. "Would you agree that whoever it is has to have magic?"

"I'd say that's the most likely scenario, yes."

"So, it's probably someone who came to Plex from another dimension."

Sebille frowned. "Or during the Rages."

We both gave her a surprised look. She shrugged. "You said it yourself, they never caught the Wizard who initiated the original Rages. Wouldn't he be the most logical person to initiate this one?"

It did make sense. "I agree. But if he's still here, he has to be really old."

"Wizards live for millennia," Sebille said. "They buy immortality through black magics."

Blood magic, I thought with a grimace. I glanced at Walt. "Do you remember why the Wizard started the initial Rages?"

"No. But my gramps might remember. Why do you ask?"

"Because if we can create a similar scenario, or at least make the Wizard believe that's what we've done, we might be able to draw him out."

"I'll buy that. But how do we spread the word once we have a plan?"

"I think I can help with that."

We all turned to look at Diandra as she limped outside to join us. She gave Sebille a bow like the one Walt had done when we'd arrived. I watched her jealously. I needed to get more bendy. "Thank you so much for healing me. I'm nearly as good as new."

Sebille nodded. "The residual aches should fade over the next couple of days. Just try to rest as much as you can."

Diandra nodded. She looked at me. "I have some ancient texts about the Dark Rages. They're written as novels to protect the information inside."

"Hidden in plain sight," I said, nodding.

"Yes. They explain the Wizard's purpose for the Rages. And we'll hopefully be able to come up with a sufficient goad to draw him in after reading them."

"Then we'll need a way to get the word out."

Diandra gazed toward her fire pit, which had been trampled and covered in fire extinguishing foam after the explosion. "I can engage a general alarm," she told us frowning. "But not without first setting some protections around my fire."

"Protections?" Sebille and I asked in unison.

Diandra nodded. "The demons didn't cause the explosion in my fire workings. They might have been sent by the same person, to distract and obscure, but my work was destroyed by someone with knowledge of how Seer magic works."

"The Wizard?" Walt asked.

"I would expect so, yes," Diandra admitted. "He

learned much during the previous Rages. And, if he still lives, I think it's safe to expect that he has been preparing for this for a long time. He'll be ready for us to try to draw him out."

"Then how are we going to do it?" Walt asked.

Sebille's long, freckled face transformed under a smile. "By attacking his ego. We're going to tell the big, bad Wizard that we don't believe in him. And that, even if we did, we'd easily be able to defeat him because he's just so yesterday's news."

Ego. The most plentiful tool in an evil genius's toolbox. "I agree with Sebille. I think that's our best option," I said.

"Good," Diandra said, nodding. "I'll start my preparations." She glanced at Walt. "If you'll come with me, I'll find the books about the Rages." She gave us a smile. "There are three of them. I'm sure you'll all enjoy the fun-filled adventure stories they contain."

Sarcasm! I thought. I had a terrible feeling I was about to engage in a marathon of uninspired and probably really boring reading.

The land far beneath his feet festered under a thick haze of ozone-scented magic, the residual fog a clear sign of how prolific his army had been in their use of black magic justice. He scoured the *land with his gaze, taking a fierce pride in its devastation. All around him, his black-clad army surged and plundered, taking by force what should have been offered freely to him and his kind.*

"Sir?" a graveled voice said from behind.

He didn't acknowledge his Sergeant's presence, knowing the man would be down on one knee, his gaze locked on the ground. His soldiers had all learned early on that the Wizard didn't care to be looked upon. His visage was one of such greatness, only a rare few could be privileged to see it. "Speak."

"The gate is open. The workings stopped. You may call your legions now."

The Wizard allowed a small smile to form on his face. High above his head, a fierce dragon, clad in the traditional black armor of the Wizard's soldiers, enveloped the fleeing opponents in magic fire, sending them into the clutches of the army that waited inside the choking fog.

"Gather the prisoners. Place them in the cells beneath this rock. And then bring her to me."

I barely kept from rolling my eyes. "A romance? Are you kidding me?"

Across the room, Sebille was draped over the only couch, her story from the Dark Rages open in front of her, and her attention riveted on its pages. She looked up, grinning. "It is a novel, Naida."

I blew air through my lips. "Are we to believe the big, bad Wizard is going to stop in the middle of his Rages and court the beautiful Princess?"

Diandra said carefully. "There are no Princesses in Plex."

We all looked at her, seeing the way her eyebrows lifted with unspoken implication. "Attend the meaning *behind* the stories."

Right, I said inside my head. *The meaning behind the stories. No romance then. At least, not a real one.* What else could it mean? Sighing wearily, I realized I'd have to keep reading to figure it out.

"Yes, Sir."

He returned his attention to the scene far below. Clenched behind him, his fingers twitched with the need to join in the fun. His energy burbled just below the surface of his skin, all but begging him to let it go. But he was saving his energies for what was to come.

And he wished for her to see it. After all, if it weren't for her, none of this would have been possible...

"**M**iss?"

My attention jerked from the book, I looked up at Hobs. "What?"

"We're bored."

I rolled my gaze over the cat, the frog, and the hobgoblin. "Go outside and play."

Hobs shook his head. "It's raining."

I narrowed my gaze on Wicked, noting the way his tail snapped behind him. He had too much energy and was looking for mischief. When my eyes met his, he jumped up onto my chair and dropped to his back, showing me his belly and then grabbing my hand between his paws and biting my fingers when I tried to scratch the downy offering. "Hey, ouch!" I complained, tugging my hand away. "Where's Kanish?"

"She's hunkered down under those trees by the house," Sebille told me without looking up.

I looked Wicked in the eyes, recognizing that he was the instigator of the current complaints. "Ask her to shelter you with her wings," I told Hobs.

The hobgoblin's blue eyes lit up at that, but his expression quickly fell. "But, where will we go, Miss?"

"I don't know," I said, wanting to get back to my book. "Why don't you go play in the caves?"

I fell back into my book, barely noticing when the trio of miscreants left.

She was a tiny thing, delicate and filled with grace, but it took two of his guards to bring her to the top of the ridge, and when they'd deposited her beside him, he'd had to use his magic to keep her from flinging herself over the edge.

The wind whipped at her verdant locks, spinning them around her pale face, so filled with defiance and a passion that looked too much like hate for his comfort.

"Observe what I have done in your name," he told the spitfire beside him.

She glared up at him, her slender form bending toward the plunging void as if she would fling herself into it through sheer will alone. "You've done nothing in my name. It has all been for you. For your pride. For your gain. You wish to control the dimensions. To create in Plex the epicenter of a nightmarish despotism. You will not stain me with this treachery. I place it at your feet where it rightly belongs."

He laughed, unaffected by her words. "Ah, but that is not how history will see it. You will be blamed for the death of your family." He pasted a sad look on his ugly face. "For the brutal murder of your unfortunate husband."

Tears sparkled in her green gaze but were forced back through ruthless will. "I will see you dead for this. For all of it. My dearest will not have died in vain. I will lay his *death at your feet along with the long list of your other treacheries."*

His laughter filled the night, sending cold terror into the hearts of his victims far below. Above him, the dense night sky roiled with a building storm. But he knew hers were the impotent words of a defeated foe. And nothing would stop him from getting everything he desired.

Nothing. And no one.

He reached out and, with a self-satisfied smile, shoved her off the rock.

"Whoa!" I said. "Okay, *not* a romance." I glanced at Walt. "Who is this chick the Wizard killed. He claimed history would blame her for everything."

Walt looked up from his book, his gaze far away. Apparently, his reading was pulling him into the past, making an impression. "I assume you mean Wilshire Montague."

"Wilshire, like your town?"

Walt nodded. "She was a Seer. One of our best and oldest magic users. Under her careful touch, Plex blossomed and grew, safe from outside interference and impermeable to evil. But then she fell in love, and her new husband wasn't quite as immune to the possibilities of evil as she was."

I nodded, pointing to the pages I'd just read. "The Wizard killed him, right?"

"Yes. And her entire family, all powerful Seers. It was passed through history that she'd killed them all in a quest for power. That she wanted the Wizard for a lover and that she killed herself when he refused her."

"Ouch," I said. "But the real story is here. Did people believe his version of events?"

"For a while, yes. It wasn't spread by him. He sent the story on the air, and it was infused within our awareness. It wasn't until he'd been gone for decades that the power of the story finally faded."

"Poor Wilshire," I murmured, staring at the page. "She'd be mighty annoyed to know the Rages were in danger of returning."

Sebille closed her book, her expression thoughtful.

"So, how did it end?" I asked the Sprite.

She sighed. "About like you'd expect. The girl dies, but not before she gets word to the Universe. The Wizard had won. He had all of the people ensnared in his magic. Anyone with any power was imprisoned in the caves of that ugly rock formation outside. But at the moment of the Seer's death, her body transformed to a message on the wind, and the message flew past the Wizard's perception, making it out into the universe."

"Unfortunately, it still took decades for the

Soldiers of Good to get past the Wizard's army and enter Plex. This history says they dropped from the sky on silver dragons and took Plex back."

"The Wizard?" Walt asked.

Sebille shrugged. "Nobody's sure. One of his guards insisted he blew himself up and disintegrated on the air to avoid being captured. But one *Soldier for Good* proclaimed he'd seen the Wizard leap on one of his black-clad dragons and fly off in the direction of the gate. His body has never been found, and no one has reported seeing him."

"I think we need to assume he's still here and still manufacturing trouble," I told them.

Sebille nodded.

I looked at Walt. "What's your book about?"

He frowned, closing the book and sitting back in his chair. His green eyes looked weary, and there were dark circles underneath them. "It covers the time after Plex was returned to the Universe. The irreversible changes to the land and the Seers who were left behind."

"Changes? What kinds of changes?"

"Well, for one, the Wizard's magic poisoned the processes of the gate. It became fickle, unpredictable, and the Seers no longer fully controlled it."

"What about the Seers?" Sebille asked.

He frowned. "That's harder to measure. Before the Rages, there were two-dozen Seer families. Their power was strong and their magics were interlinked like a complex puzzle. But the Wizard's magic made subtle changes to the links, corrupting them so that they no longer fit tightly together."

"Which is why the gate magics no longer worked," Sebille speculated.

Walt shrugged. "Maybe. Though scholars aren't sure if that was the case, or if it worked the other way around."

"That their magic didn't work because the gate was corrupt," I said, nodding. "Chicken or egg..."

Walt looked confused by my analogy but didn't ask for clarification. "Some of the families began to die off as if the imperfections in their magics were killing them. Others lost their magic entirely. As the years rolled past, their legacy was erased as thoroughly as if it had never been."

"But some of the families must have kept their magic?" I said. "You still had Seers."

"Yes. ten families." His expression turned sad. "Now, many of those are gone too."

"I can't believe their disappearance is just a coincidence," I said. "It has to be tied to what's going on with the dimensional breach."

"I agree," he said. "But I couldn't tell you how."

"Is it possible one of the remaining Seers used the remnants of the Wizard's magic to enhance their power?" Sebille asked.

"I guess it's possible," Walt agreed. "Or that one of them was actually working with him all along. But if that's the case, the individual has stayed dormant for a long time. What would have spurred the changes now?"

We sat in thought for a long moment, staring into the blazing fire Diandra had built to stave off the chill of the stormy night outside.

The door opened and I jumped, turning to find Diandra with her arms filled with wood for the fire. She slid a speculative glance over us. "Finished?"

We nodded. Walt jumped up to grab the wood from her, organizing it into a neat pile on the hearth.

"Good. I've made stew. We can talk about it over our meal."

I suddenly realized Wicked and gang hadn't come back yet. Sighing unhappily, I realized I was going to have to trudge out into the cold, rainy night to find them. Glancing at the others, I said, "I'll go fetch the children."

Sebille and I shared a smile.

To my surprise, she stood too. "I'll go with you."

16

DANK, DARK MAGIC

*a*s we stepped out into the night, a cold, wet breeze flashed past, filled with the sour stench of an old fire. I tugged my muddy, tattered coat around me, wishing the little hut had a washing machine. My gaze slid to Diandra's working fire, seeing only a vaguely circular black stain on the ground.

"It's a good thing you showed up when you did. The Seer was burned pretty badly."

Sebille held out a hand, suffused with a gentle green illumination to light our way. "My energy feels different here."

I nodded. "Mine is much stronger. It has some-thing to do with the fact that it's a non-magical place, I think."

She didn't respond, so I glanced her way. "What?"

"Nothing. I was just wondering if it was more than that. This place..." she swept a hand around us, encompassing everything hidden by the darkness. "It doesn't feel empty of magic. If anything, it feels almost too full."

I thought about it, throwing out my sensing magics and feeling a thickness throbbing on the air that hadn't been there before. Or, at least it hadn't been there in Wilshire Plex. I hadn't really tested it since arriving at the border. "Maybe you're feeling the dimensional gate."

"Maybe." She squinted into the darkness. "*That's* where you sent the kids to play?"

The black exterior of the rocky ridge rose high above us, the craggy rock looking like a demonic face in the rainy dark. It definitely looked more foreboding at night.

"It didn't look so intimidating earlier."

As we started off, I turned to her and asked, "Did you find out what happened to Rustin and Sadie?"

She nodded, looking unhappy. "They're okay. It's like I suspected, Madeline pulled them back when she felt Rustin losing energy. I got her to promise she wouldn't hurt Sadie, and I told her I'd like to keep her."

"Do you think she'll honor that promise?"

"Yeah. She's scary, but she adores her niece and Maude made her promise, so..."

We approached a large opening in roughly the

center of the ridge. Its outline looked as if it had been cut from the rock by hand. As we approached, I added my own gentle glow to Sebille's, scouring the ground in front of the opening for hobgoblin and cat-like prints.

I saw only a mash of mud and puddles, with one enormous print that clearly belonged to Kanish. "They're definitely in there," I told Sebille, as if she'd voiced concern that they weren't. It wasn't until that moment that I realized I'd been a little concerned myself.

We stepped inside, and it felt as if we'd stepped into a different world.

The cold damp of the exterior gave way to bone-deep arctic temps that had my teeth chattering within moments. A grave-like cold.

The air smelled stale and dusty, filled with scents from long ago that had been trapped by the thick rock walls. The silence was the worst aspect. It was a deep, unnatural silence that pulsed against my skin, bringing with it a feeling of hopelessness that made me want to cry.

"I can't believe you sent them here," Sebille said, glaring over at me.

I grimaced but didn't try to defend myself. There really was no defense. "We need to find them." Irrational fear overwhelmed me. My heart pounded against my ribs, my mind playing dire music that would have been right at home in a gore-filled horror movie. I took off nearly running without a plan beyond finding Wicked, Slimy, and Hobs and scuttling safely out of that terrible place.

Sebille caught up with me, grabbing my arm and wrenching me to a halt. Her iridescent green eyes glowed softly. They were unusually wide, and her lips were pinched. She rested her forehead against mine and spoke in a whisper. "We're being watched."

I lifted my head and looked around, the panic that had sent me scurrying tripling within the beat of a heart. "Where!"

"Shhhh!" Sebille tugged my arm with hurtful fingers. "They're everywhere and nowhere. Don't let them know we see them."

The ridiculousness of that statement sliced through my instinctual fear. I frowned. "But we *don't* see them. At least, I don't. Do you?"

Sebille's gaze slid over the walls, her hand lifting to shine light over the dry, craggy surface. We were surrounded on all sides by rock. The space was circular, like a well.

I frowned, fear tearing at me with razor-sharp claws. "How'd we get inside a well."

"Miss?"

Our heads shot up, up, up, and we saw Hobs' big blue eyes staring down at us, the shock of light brown hair between his ears bobbing with his movements. "What are you doing down there?"

Sebille and I looked at each other. I could tell

from her expression that she, like me, had no idea how we'd gotten there.

I shrugged. "I don't know, Hobs. We weren't here a minute ago. Where's Wicked?"

"Meow!"

The sound reverberated around us, coming from everywhere and nowhere at once. A shadow moved low on one wall, the form familiar and sleek. Like my cat, the form had a long tail that whipped the air behind him. "Wicked?" I rushed over, finding only a shadow sliding over the rocky surface. "Where are you?"

"You know you really shouldn't have sent us in here by ourselves," the frog said. I glanced toward Sebille and saw Slimy's face superimposed over hers. Unlike normal, his froggy lips moved when he spoke. Though, the judgy tone he was using was pure Sebille. "What kind of mother sends her children into an ancient prison filled with dark magical influences?"

I stared into the bulgy, judgy black eyes. "I...I'm not your mother."

Yeah, that really was the best I could come up with. But in my defense, things were a bit upside down and backward.

Fire shot past high over Hobs' head. Kanish's leonine head appeared above him. Her beautiful, slanted gaze peered down at us, a gleam filling them that made me uncomfortable. I watched in horror as the dragon's wide maw opened, revealing a deadly mouth full of sharp, ripping teeth. She lowered the teeth toward Hobs, who seemed strangely oblivious to her presence there.

I tried to scream his name, terror making it impossible as the air locked in my chest. Hobs and Kanish disappeared.

A sharp crack made Sebille and me jump. A second cracking sound was louder, and went on much longer, as the walls around us began to fracture and fall away, raining down on us as we stood helpless in the center of the space, with nothing to do but hold our arms over our heads.

A horrendous groaning sound drew my gaze upward, and I barely had time to scream before the bulk of the rock wall fell onto us.

I woke up to the icy fall of rain on my face. My back ached. My arms and legs felt weak, too drained to move.

I opened my eyes, squinting against the constant fall of rain. The liquid hit my eyes and burned, making it nearly impossible to keep them open.

But I forced them open anyway, the feeling that were weren't alone making me uncomfortable.

He wore a dark robe, the hood completely

covering his face, and was flinging dust into a fire that burned brightly despite the torrential rains.

I shoved to my elbows, looking around. We were on top of the ridge. The same ridge where the Wizard and poor Wilshire Montague had their last conversation. Gritting my teeth, I pushed to a sitting position, my hand brushing up against something warm and squishy.

Sebille was stretched out beside me, her bright red hair glowing through the dark. I felt for her pulse and found it strong and steady.

But she was out.

"Who are you? What's going on? Where are my friends?"

The man in the robe continued to throw dust into the fire, sending multi-hued flame into the air around him. Smoke billowed up to the sky, but I couldn't smell it. And I realized the Seer wasn't real either. He was simply another vision brought on by the residual magic of the caves.

We needed to get out of there.

But as I stood, The Seer at the fire said, "Between your hopes and expectations."

I turned back. If he could talk to me, maybe I could talk to him. I really needed some answers. "Who's manipulating the dimensional gate? How do I stop him?"

The man continued to fling dust into the fire for long enough that I didn't think he was going to respond. Then his head slowly lifted. I saw dark eyes under a greasy fringe of hair above a grungy face. "Between your hopes and expectations." He tugged a pocket watch from his robes, poking at it with a thick, dusty digit. "Time is precious. Guard it well."

And he disappeared.

"Miss?"

Hands shook my shoulders.

"Miss? Wake up."

A distant rumbling sound wove its way into my dreams, the sound like a beacon calling me back to consciousness.

"Ahhhhhhhhhhh!"

The goat! I'd forgotten about Adelaide. I always forgot about poor Adelaide.

I moved, dust flaring up around me, and sneezed so hard it wrenched me awake. "Ugh!" I groaned, rolling to my side. "What hit me?"

Hobs twisted his lips to the side. "Sorry, Miss. It was the only way to wake you up."

"Meow," Wicked said. He jumped onto my chest, looking down at me. "Meow?"

"I'm okay, buddy. I think."

"Gargoyle goobers," Sebille groaned beside me. "What hit me?"

Hobs' oversized head seemed to sink into his scrawny shoulders.

"It wasn't you, Hobs," I told him. "It was dark

magic." I looked at the Sprite. "Did you see the guy in the robes?"

Her expression clearly showed her confusion. "No. Worse. I spoke to Madeline."

"Quilleran?" I asked, shocked. "What did she say?"

"Gobbledygook. Something about being between expectations."

"Between your hopes and expectations?" I asked.

She nodded. "Yeah, that was it. Like I said, gobbledygook."

"I'm not so sure about that." I pushed to my feet. "Come on, we need to go talk to Walt."

"I told you, I don't know what it means," Walt said. "Nobody understands the Seer's proclamations."

I shook my head. "Just because you don't understand them doesn't mean they aren't important."

Walt frowned.

I stared at him for a moment, seeing the lie sliding through his gaze. "You've been living with a secret for a long time, haven't you, Walt?"

Everyone looked at me, a question in their gazes. But Walt wouldn't lift his gaze to mine. He was staring determinedly at the floor.

"You suspected the truth when you read the

histories, didn't you? You didn't want to face it, but it was always there, nudging you, helping you out of difficult situations."

"What are you talking about?" Diandra asked, frowning.

"Magic," Sebille said, her bright, green gaze sliding to mine. "He's a descendant."

Walt flinched as if struck. "No."

"Yes, Walt," I told him gently. "The green hair and green eyes are a dead giveaway. All Seers have them. It's a trait implying magic." I knew that only because of the history I'd read. The knowledge had never been dispersed to the general public. Walt's friends and neighbors wouldn't know unless they spent time at the gate, around the other Seers. And that was just never done.

Sebille slowly lifted her gaze to Diandra and the other woman flinched. She grabbed a strand of her red hair. "It's dyed. I like red."

Sebille narrowed her eyes but returned her attention to me.

Walt shook his head again, still refusing to look at me.

"You shoved the magic away. Your family wanted nothing to do with it, did they? They didn't want the responsibility. They knew there was danger involved. And the Wizard was still out there, somewhere. Being a distant relative of Wilshire Montague's would be like a neon sign over your heads. You didn't want the Wizard to find you."

A moment passed before Walt lifted his head. I pulled air into my lungs in a surprised gasp as his black gaze fell onto mine. So quickly I could have convinced myself I'd imagined it, he blinked and the magic fell away, leaving only the grassy green of his natural gaze behind. He sighed. "It burns beneath my skin, calls to me. The magic is a gift. It has no business being repressed."

I nodded. "You've always wanted to pursue your destiny, haven't you? You wanted to tell your parents, your grandparents, that you were going to fulfill the legacy they'd rejected. But they begged you... pleaded with you not to do it. And you knew it would bring the Wizard down on their heads if you did. All of them. Old and young alike, would die under his hand."

Walt slid a gaze toward Diandra. Her gaze was a glossy, terrifying black. "I'm sorry," he told her.

She gave her head a little shake. "You have a goddess-given calling. You hid behind fear and left the danger to others. You're disgusting." The Seer turned and walked out into the night, rage visible in every line of her slight body.

Walt shook his head. "She doesn't understand. No one who has never had a family would understand. I'd do anything to protect them."

I wondered how many others in Plex had gone

underground after the Dark Rages. How many others had done what Seers don't generally do...had large families, lived normal, happy lives without the threat of death and destruction hanging over their heads?

I shook my head. "I get it, Walt. But now we have a problem. I suspect the Wizard knows you're a latent Seer. Despite your not showing any interest to serve, he knows. And he's probably been watching your family closely. He'll know you've come to the gate."

I stared at him for a long moment, waiting for him to understand. When his face paled, I saw that he knew. "My family!"

I glanced at Sebille. "We need to go to Wilshire Plex."

She nodded. "I can fly, the dragon can carry you and Walt."

Walt was already running. He threw open the door, and the brittle wind threw icy rain at us as we stepped out into it.

A small figure stood in the rain, the wind whipping her robes violently around her legs. Her glossy, black gaze lifted to Walt's and magic flared around us, a violent wash against the already fierce tempest of the storm.

17

INTO A WORLD OF BLINDING WHITE LIGHT

*D*iandra stared at Walt, her body stiff and unyielding. Time stopped around us, even the storm fell away as their magic formed a cocoon that muted the rest of the world.

I lifted my hands, prepared to use whatever magic I had at my disposal to stop them from fighting. I had no idea if Diandra was the Wizard's toy, or if she was simply a victim of his machinations, but I knew she was much more experienced in the use of Seer magics than Walt was.

He wouldn't have a chance against her.

"Diandra, you need to calm down," I told her, stepping between her and Walt.

But he set me gently aside. "This is my fight, Keeper. For once, I must take responsibility for my actions and engage."

Another tense moment throbbed between us.

Wicked wound around my calves, purring loudly, and then moved past me to curl himself around the Seer's legs before sliding around Walt's ankles and then sitting on my feet. He was a warm, rumbling weight that reassured.

And he'd apparently used his dousing magics to bring calm to a moment fraught with deadly tension.

Diandra blinked, expelling the black from her eyes. Moisture glistened on her lashes, and it wasn't from the rain. "I'm a hypocrite, she told Walt. I berate you for not fulfilling your duty, yet I am guilty of the same crime." She looked down at her clasped hands, covered in glistening raindrops. "I knew where he'd taken them, yet I did nothing. I hid within the safety of my hut and ignored the shifting of the dimensional barrier. Three shiftings I've ignored. Because I feared his retribution if I did anything to stop it." She shook her head, sniffling. "I've been a coward and don't have the excuse of doing it to save loved ones. I have no loved ones. I have nothing." She lifted her gaze to Walt's again. "But you have people who depend on you to keep them safe. I will help you do that. If you'll allow me to."

The panic that had been twisting my belly eased. I took a deep breath, realizing I hadn't breathed for too long.

Walt hesitated a few beats and then nodded. "I'd be honored for your help, Seer Diandra."

She closed her eyes for a moment, clearly relieved by his response, and then nodded briskly. "We do not need the dragon. I know how to get there quickly. Please, follow me."

———————

We stood in front of the entrance to the caves. My heart was pounding so hard I could feel it in my throat. My feet didn't want to move forward.

Walt and Diandra stopped, looking back at us with a question in their eyes. I couldn't voice the pervasive, oily fear that saturated me as I looked into the void beyond the opening.

Sebille was uncharacteristically quiet, her lean body tense beside mine.

Even Hobs stood behind me, one hand clutching my shirt as if he planned to shove me at the monster when it leaped out at us.

Problem was, the monster wasn't a physical thing I could battle. It was amorphous, ethereal, undefined. And it was power personified.

"What's wrong?" Diandra asked.

I blinked and shook my head. "I don't think I can go back in there."

In my hands, Slimy shivered violently, his blank black eyes bulging even more than usual. "There's magic in front of the door."

It took a minute for his words to sink in. I looked down at him. "Door?"

"The green one. It's covered in shimmering, black magic."

I looked at Diandra. She nodded. "Yes, the door's the portal."

I narrowed my gaze, peering past her. "Can you see a door in there?"

She pointed to the solid rock wall. "It's right here."

Sebille and I shared a look. I knew what she was thinking. We'd stepped through the entrance before, and then everything had gone wonky. Even before we'd had a chance to see what the cave contained.

"We got caught up in some kind of magical hypnosis before," Sebille told the Seer. "We weren't able to control anything. And we ended up there." She pointed toward the top of the rocky ridge. "I have no idea how."

Diandra frowned thoughtfully. "I see. Maybe it's because your energies are foreign to the cave. It's probably been spelled to protect the portal." She cocked her head, eyeing Slimy. "The frog can see the door?"

"He's magic sensitive," I told her. "Sometimes, he sees things we don't see."

The night behind us flared with heat and light. A thick shaft of yellow-gold flame seared the air. We turned to find Kanish standing way too close, given her size and the range of her fire.

She roared, painting us in smoky heat.

I looked at Walt.

"She says she can block the illusion. We need to take her with us."

Diandra shook her head. "The dragon won't fit through the door."

"She will," Slimy said. "It will expand."

The Seer eyed the frog, her pretty face filled with doubt. Then she shrugged. "If she gets stuck, I'm not sure we'll be able to release her."

Looking at the dragon, Walt belched out a human-sized roar of dragonish and Kanish sent fire into the sky in response, flapping her wings.

Water sprayed over us as Kanish moved her wings, drenching our clothes.

"Dripping dragon goobers," I cursed softly, brushing at the raindrops on my clothes.

Diandra turned and headed into the cave. As soon as she took a step inside, she disappeared.

Walt stepped inside before I could stop him.

Sebille, Hobs, and I shared a look. We were all afraid to risk it again.

But the dragon stepped forward, towering over us as she covered us with a still-dripping wing. As soon as her wings surrounded us, I could see the two Seers inside. Diandra was kneeling on the ground, chanting, her hands uplifted, palms upward and a tiny purple flame burning in each one.

Walt had his eyes closed and was chanting with her. His fingers twitched at his sides. After a few seconds, fire flared up from his palms, though I didn't think he noticed.

A moment later, light flickered behind the portal, showing in the fine cracks between the door and the frame. The portal slowly eased open, and the two Seers walked through. Into a world of glowing white light. We followed quickly, not wanting to be left behind.

We stepped into the light only a moment behind Walt and Diandra, relieved that Kanish had been right. Her magic had repelled the dark magic of the cave. Unfortunately, the dragon did indeed become wedged, giving off a deep grunt and a cloud of pale gray smoke as her sides hit the frame of the door and stuck.

We watched as she struggled to pull herself free, concern building as the moment stretched to two and then three. I looked at Sebille. She shrugged. "I can douse her with shrinking energy, but I'm not sure how it would interact with the dragon's own magic."

I looked down at Slimy. He looked up at me but didn't say anything. *Yeah, act like a dumb frog and pretend you didn't just promise us the dragon would fit through the door*, I thought at him.

He blinked and stiffened.

Trickle, trickle, trickle.

"Oh no, you didn't!" I said.

I was pretty sure I heard the frog chuckle as I grabbed him with my un-peed-on hand and wiped my other hand on the spiky grass beneath my feet.

There was an ominous creaking sound.

I felt my eyes go wide.

The dragon grunted, visibly straining to get through the door.

The creaking turned to a groan and then a screech as the big reptile bent the frame of the magical door.

I was opening my mouth to comment that we needed to try something to help when the door suddenly expanded and the dragon shot through like a bullet, heading right for us.

Our screams were quickly smacked out of us by about five thousand pounds of reptile banging against us, flinging us sideways. Kanish lifted her wings and took off flying as if she hadn't just been pooped from a magical door, and left us behind.

I hit the ground and skidded several feet, smacking up against a scrubby bush that felt as if it was covered in sharp needles. The frog flew out of my hand when I hit, leaving behind a few more trickles of frog incontinence as he flew over my head.

I grimaced, wiping my hand on the grass again.

"I don't really blame you for that one," I told him as I climbed to my feet, groaning. Every bone in my body felt bruised.

A muffled croak was the only response I got from the frog.

In the distance, I heard a heartfelt scream of, "Again!" and knew Hobbs was okay.

I tried to peer through the oppressive light to see my assistant. "Sebille?"

My ears buzzed. I shook my head, trying to remember if I'd smacked it when I'd been tossed like a well-used tissue.

The buzzing didn't stop.

A big bug shot past my ear and I swung at it, earning myself a Sprite-style barrage of cursing for my trouble.

"Hey, watch out, you gnish! I didn't barely escape with my life from the giant dragon projectile only to be squashed by you."

"Then don't buzz me like that," I groused back. "It's annoying."

The sound of the portal door slamming closed sliced our argument short and jettisoned us into a fun new experience.

Pure, unadulterated darkness.

18

THE GOBLIN-CURSED PLACE

I sat where I was for a long moment. Listening. Trying to get my bearings.

The buzzing stopped, telling me Sebille had either left or she was no longer Sprite-sized. My vision started to adjust after a bit, and I realized the previously bright light had skewed my night vision. My other senses kicked in and I heard the heavy throb of dragon wings on the air.

Kanish was coming back. I rolled to my knees. "Slimy?"

"Ribbit."

"Oh no! Please don't tell me I knocked the ability to speak right out of you again?"

"Ribbit?"

"He's just messin' with ya," a voice said through the darkness.

"Naida? Is that you?"

I shoved to my feet. "I'm looking for the frog."

A green light appeared out of the darkness, showing Sebille holding Hobs' hand three feet away from me.

High above us, Kanish released another bolt of dragon fire, temporarily illuminating the spot where we stood. Wicked bounced over, tail high and ears forward, and rubbed his forehead on my shins. "Hey, buddy. I'm glad you're okay."

"Where's the frog?" Sebille asked.

I shook my head. "He's not talking to me."

Wicked trotted around the bush that had *sort of* cushioned my landing and sounded a warning, "Meow!"

"Stop messing around, Slimy," I told the frog. "I'm not mad at you for peeing on me...twice."

"In my defense," said the frog in his snotty voice, "It was like being shot out of a canon. It was terrifying. I'm not exactly built for rough and tumble antics," he whined.

"I beg to differ," said Sebille. "You've got plenty of protective padding."

We smacked palms, grinning.

"Very funny, Sprite," sayeth the frog.

"Where in Cinderella's pointy glass slippers did the Seers go?" I asked, looking around.

Kanish roared, spitting more fire into the air, but our translator was missing. "Sorry, girl. I have no idea what you're saying."

The dragon hovered above our heads, body slightly vertical and wings throbbing slowly to keep her afloat. She dipped her elegant head and whipped around on the air, heading away from us.

"I think she wants us to follow, Miss," Hobs said.

Since my cat was already bounding after the dragon, it was a simple decision to go after her. Scooping up the frog, I handed him to Sebille. "It's your turn to be peed on," I told her.

She grimaced, holding him away from her with the tips of her fingers.

"Ha," fake-laughed the frog. "You know I have feelings, right?"

"If you don't want to be razzed, then stop piddling on me," I told him.

I thought that was an entirely reasonable request.

———

The ground was hard, rocky, and there was very little vegetation. The occasional scrubby tree or spiky bush provided the only "softness" in an otherwise bleak and shadowy landscape.

And it was cold.

So cold.

Sebille had tucked the frog inside her shirt, against her body, with a threat that if he peed on her she was going to dump him on the ground and leave him to freeze.

I had my arms wrapped around myself and was considering calling Kanish down to fire up a spiky bush or two for warmth.

I'd ditched my coat at the hut, not realizing we'd be heading into colder climes, and my light-weight sweater and muddy jeans were useless in that kind of cold.

Hobbs didn't seem to feel the cold like I did, he'd wrapped the length of his Christmas sweater around his upper body and he seemed happy, his bare feet and hands not even purple like mine were.

Of course, Sebille had come to Plex better equipped for all types of weather. She was wearing several layers, furry boots, and had a scarf around her throat and gloves on her hands.

In my defense, I hadn't been planning on being sucked into Plex and therefore hadn't had a chance to prepare. Still, I really could have used that burlap bag. If I'd had it at hand, I'd have pulled a snowsuit and a few tacos out faster than Hobs could squeal, "Again!".

Not necessarily in that order. Just for grins, I sent my keeper energy out into the night, watching the silvery threads swirl away from me and disappear. When there was no clang of discovery, I sighed.

No burlap bag for me.

High above our heads, the dragon suddenly

roared. She dipped her nose and lunged toward the ground.

"It looks like she's found them," I told Sebille, shivering so hard my teeth clacked together.

Taking pity on me, Sebille tugged off her outer layer, a form-fitting fleece jacket, and handed it to me. She still had on a turtleneck under a sweatshirt, and probably a layer beneath that. "Thank you!" I pulled it on gratefully, sighing at the almost immediate warmth.

"Don't drool on it or anything."

Would it have killed her just to be nice?

I snorted at my unspoken question. The answer was a resounding yes. She would have fallen into the fetal position and died on the spot.

Wicked came bounding back and met us on the trail, he was no longer purring, and his tail was whipping the air with the type of violence that told me something was very wrong.

"What is it, buddy?"

Lightning sheered across the sky, illuminating a craggy landscape and a distant, snow-covered peak. I suddenly realized where I was. But I didn't have time to figure out what it meant before the lightning sliced downward like a guided missile and exploded the ground.

I shrieked, the concussive force of the blast blowing me backward and up, and something popped inside my ears.

I flew through the air and landed in a foggy puddle several feet away. Confused and feeling like someone had pounded me flat with a giant meat tenderizer, I lay there for several moments, taking stock. Voices murmured around me, dulled and indecipherable. There was a short, sharp scream that filled me with an unanswered urgency to pull myself together and drag myself upright.

But the longer I lay there, the more painful areas I identified in my body.

A burning sensation ripped at my insides. From out of my murky thoughts came the sudden, panicked surety that I'd been struck by lightning and my insides were on fire.

Pain throbbed in my fingertips, accompanied by an angry sizzling sound.

I battled terror, discomfort, and the fog in my brain and forced my eyes open.

Panic roared through me. I couldn't see!

Then I realized the problem. I shoved hair out of my eyes, yelping as lightning zapped my face. No. Not lightning. My own energy.

The world spun around me, making me roll to my side and retch. I was dizzy. So dizzy. And my power was burning in my belly to get out. In the distance, there was screaming. Prolonged, pain-filled screaming.

Then I remembered my friends. "Wicked?" I

pushed to a seated position, fighting nausea as I looked around. "Sebille? Hobbs? Slimy?"

Sebille groaned, her upper body suddenly appearing a few feet away from behind a tree as she sat up. Her eyes went crossed and she threw a hand over her mouth, retching into the grass.

"Miss?" Hobs' voice was weak, and I couldn't see him.

"Hobs! Where are you?"

"I'm over here..." He coughed wetly. His voice held no joy. No excitement. No demand for more. That was when I knew he was in trouble. "Keep talking so I can find you."

"I'm with Mr. Wicked. He's..." Hobs coughed again, leaving me clinging with horror to his hanging sentence. "He's what, Hobs! Keep talking..."

"He's not moving, Miss Naida."

Oh goddess, no! He had to be all right. If he wasn't... Rage boiled in my chest and the burning sensation increased in my belly as my magic tried to escape its confines. My power had recognized we were under attack and wanted to be let out to deal with it.

The world shimmied, dipped, and I nearly passed out again. I shook my head to clear it, forcing myself to my knees. "I'm coming, Hobs."

"Teeny tiny amphibian diapers, frog!" Sebille exclaimed. "I can't believe you pooped on me!"

I saw Hobs up ahead. He was bending over the

small, unmoving form of my cat. "No, no, no, no, no..." I chanted as I tried to stand, nearly falling over from another wave of dizziness. I stayed on my knees and crawled toward Wicked, praying he'd be okay. "Sebille!" I screamed as I reached my little man. "Wicked's hurt. I need you."

There was blood on the fur around his ears. His eyes were open, but he wasn't moving. I quickly checked to make sure he was breathing.

Sebille stumbled over, falling to her knees beside him. "Give me some room, Naida."

I tried to move away, I really did, but terror had me firmly in its grip and my limbs wouldn't obey my mind's instructions.

I leaned back slightly though, and looked at Hobs. He had a thin stream of blood running down one leg, and his knee looked slightly swollen, but I didn't see any other damage. "Are you okay, Hobs?"

He nodded, his big blue eyes filled with tears. "Is he...?"

Sebille's hands lit up, a soft glow that bathed Wicked's entire body in green. My cat trembled once, violently, and then went still. A beat later, he trembled again. Then again, until his entire body succumbed to convulsions.

"Sebille?"

She didn't look up. Her eyes were closed, and she was chanting softly.

I knew I should shut up and let her do her work, but I just couldn't. "Sebille!"

The glow increased, thickening to the point where Wicked's small, still form disappeared beneath Sebille's potent earth energy.

Lightning seared the night again, but it shot upward into the sky, slamming into Kanish and sending her shrieking toward the ground in a trail of helpless smoke and flame.

I bit back a scream, realizing we were under a coordinated attack, and it would be really stupid to announce our location.

Not that the Wizard didn't already know where we were since he'd just hit us with a direct line of power.

I stared at the thick green wash of energy covering my sweet, beautiful cat, tears sliding from my eyes. He had to be okay. He just had to be.

My heart pounded against my ribs. Terror blossomed in my chest, fed by my hammering pulse. And I knew with the certainty of death that Wicked was far from okay.

"Sebille..." I whispered, beyond desperate.

The Sprite sagged downward, her eyes remaining closed as she fell back onto her butt on the dirt and then onto her back.

She'd given him everything she had.

I reached for her, clasping her icy hand in silent

thanks. However it turned out, I owed her a great debt for what she'd tried to do.

Sebille's hand was slack in mine. Her skin was clammy, and the freckles on her pale face nearly glowed against the paleness of her skin.

Had I killed the Sprite asking her to save Wicked?

Stars burst before my eyes and I wobbled on my knees, the edges of my vision going dark. I was a single heartbeat away from passing out again.

"Miss?" Hobs' hand clasped my shoulder, his touch bringing me back from the edge.

"I'm okay," I told him. But it was a lie. I was about as far from okay as I could be.

Movement caught my peripheral vision. My gaze snapped to Wicked, and I saw with relief that he was moving. The tightrope of tension in my chest eased. I gave a small sound of pure joy as Mr. Wicked tried to stand. His eyes rolled back for a beat and then refocused. After a beat, Wicked struggled to his feet and shook himself, falling over again under the violence of the movement. I grabbed him up, holding him close as he purred.

"Thank the goddess," I murmured.

"Thank the Sprite," Sebille answered in a rusty voice.

I laughed wetly, brushing snot from under my nose.

"We need to move. He just took Kanish down," I told her. "I know you're spent, but..."

She sighed, nodding. "Come on, I saw a cave not too far away. We can take cover and form a plan. If we just continue to stumble on the way we've been doing, we're all going to be fuzzy splats on the ground of this goblin-cursed place."

19

THE PLAN VS THE EXECUTION

"We have to assume Walt and Diandra are working against him, wherever they are," I told my friends. Sebille didn't look entirely convinced, but she nodded.

"They're going to have their hands full," Sebille said. "Walt doesn't have a clue what he's doing as a Seer. I doubt he'd even be able to drum up any defensive magic right now. Which means it's really Diandra's show."

"He can amplify her energies like he did in the cave."

Sebille nodded. "That will help. But he's going to need us." She looked around, her gaze narrowing on the frog. "Even the incontinent frog."

"Hey!" Slimy objected.

I fought a grin. "Maybe Mr. Slimy can distract the Wizard by pooping on him."

"Har!" the frog said.

Sebille bent over the sandy ground, the stick in her hand creating swirls and arrows over the battle plan we'd begun. "First, we find Kanish and make sure she's okay..."

———

As plans went, it was disastrously weak. We were going to need all the luck we could get, especially since the Wizard appeared to be a lot more powerful than we were, and always seemed to be several steps ahead of us. The fact that we still hadn't found Walt or Diandra worried me.

A lot.

They'd been only seconds ahead of us through the door. Granted, we'd lost a couple of minutes waiting for Kanish to unwedge herself, but we hadn't been *that* far behind them. I couldn't shake the feeling they'd been grabbed by the Wizard a soon as they came through the door. And if that was true, I had to wonder why he'd let us roam. He obviously didn't think we were much of a threat.

I was going to do my best to change his mind about that.

Ahead of us, smoke rose in a curling ribbon from a dark mound on the ground. "There she is," I whispered. I called the dragon's name softly as we approached, not wanting her to attack us before she realized who we were.

Kanish lifted her long head from the ground, peering at us through pain-filled eyes. Her chest rumbled and smoke wafted from her flared nostrils.

Her wings were outstretched and looked slightly crumpled. Not a good sign. Dragons generally folded their wings against their bodies when they were at rest.

If she wasn't tucking them up, they were probably broken.

I glanced at Sebille, wondering if she had it in her to heal the dragon. Frowning, I really wished we were home, so we'd have more resources.

An explosion in the distance sent dirt and rock geysering into the sky. Flames flared up behind the explosion, and I realized not all of the smoke wafting over the ground had come from Kanish. "There's a battle nearby. Walt and Diandra are fighting him," I told Sebille as she knelt beside the dragon and ran her hands over the creature's heaving sides. A soft, green glow beneath her palms told me she was assessing the big reptile for damage.

She sent me a worried glance. "Broken ribs, several of them." She glanced at the crumpled wings. "That's going to take a lot of energy to fix."

I sighed, realizing what had to be done. We needed to scrap our carefully thought-out plan. "Okay," I said. "Plan B. You're going to have to stay here. Once Kanish is on her feet again, you two can join us." I knew there was a good chance Sebille's energy stores would be so depleted she'd be of limited use in the battle, but the dragon's help might be vital and I had no choice anyway. "Hobs can stay here and watch your back."

"No, Miss!" the hobgoblin whined. "I need to help."

"You *would* be helping..." I started to tell him, knowing in my heart he was right. I really needed his help.

"I'll stay," Slimy interrupted. "I can't fight anyway. But I can be useful as an extra pair of eyes."

I looked at Sebille. She nodded. "They're right. The frog is a better choice to stay with me. You're going to need all the help you can get."

I sighed. "Take care of yourself...and Mr. Pooper there."

Sebille chuckled, some of the weariness leaving her face. "Worst case, I'll hand him to the Wizard and yell Boo! That should be enough for the frog to release all of his biologicals and send the Wizard screaming into the night."

"You two are a laugh riot," said the frog.

I was still chuckling as I headed toward the fire-fight in the distance. I mean, why not? It might be the last time I ever got to laugh at the frog's expense. I might as well enjoy the heck out of it.

The ground exploded not thirty feet away from us, flinging debris into our faces in a stinging cloud. We hit the ground, Hobs and I covering our heads and me yanking Wicked beneath me to protect him. Coughing violently, I lifted my head again, seeing the line of gray smoke hanging in the air.

I watched another bolt of energy emerge from the rocky ridge a hundred yards away and hit the pocked and torn ground about ten yards from where it had last hit. Small fires formed a rough arc showing the area the Wizard had been targeting and, in the very center of that area, a slender form bent over a tiny fire behind a large boulder, shoulders rounded and head low.

Diandra!

I motioned to Hobs. He took off in a blur of movement. A beat later the Seer yelped, throwing up her hands and falling over as the timbers in her fire blew into the air and settled back, the flames shooting higher than before.

A gust of wind was the only warning I got that he was back. "It's only her," Hobs said. "I circled the whole area and didn't see Walt."

My stomach tightened. My theory was apparently accurate. Walt must have been grabbed as soon as they came through the portal. Though I had no idea how Diandra had avoided the same fate.

There was only one way to find out. I called out to her. "Diandra, it's Naida. We're coming in."

The Seer spun in surprise when I first spoke, her curved fingers spitting energy that was too black to see except for the silver glare of the sparks it gave off. She relaxed her stance and dropped her hands, falling back to a squat over the fire.

We hurried over, and I dropped into a crouch next to her. "Where's Walt?"

She skimmed me a quick look, her expression dire. "The Wizard has him. I tried to get to him as soon as I realized the Wizard was there, but the evil one was too fast. He touched Walt and they were both gone in a flash of light."

I rubbed my face. "I'm surprised he didn't take you."

She frowned. "I've been thinking about that. I think he took Walt because of who he is, rather than the fact that he's a Seer." She fixed me with a look. "The Wizard has Walt's family."

My knees buckled, and I dropped to my butt into the dirt. "Oh no." My mind formed a picture of all the happy Walt-like faces around the table. All those siblings. The baby... "We have to save them," I told Diandra.

She jerked her chin toward the fire. "That's what I'm doing here. But I could use some help."

"What can I do?" I asked.

She grabbed a handful of dust from somewhere inside her robe, flinging it on the fire and examining the results carefully. Then she lifted her gaze. "I think his family is there." She pointed toward a dark slash in the rock at the far end of the ridge.

An icy sense of foreboding filled me as I remembered what it had been like to enter the caves at the border. The two ridges looked a lot alike. I figured that wasn't a coincidence.

"Can you take whoever you have with you and get the Mongs out? I'll keep the Wizard distracted until Walt's family is safe, and then we'll focus on stopping the evil one."

I glanced at Wicked and Hobs, dread filling me. But I couldn't say no. I'd read the historical account of the Mage killing Wilshire Montague. I knew he was ruthless, as well as a cold-blooded killer. "Of course," I said. "How will I let you know when I've got them out?"

She thought about it for a moment. "Send energy into the air, straight up to the sky. I'll know it's you by your energy signature."

I nodded and took off running, really wishing I had Sebille and Kanish with me as backup.

We didn't take the direct route. I sent Hobs ahead to scout out the safest route to the cave I could no longer see because we were approaching it from the side instead of head-on.

He was back a beat later, pointing toward a large copse of scrubby-needled trees about twenty yards ahead. "There." Then he shot toward the trees again, my cat tearing off after him.

I bent over, lowering my profile as much as I could, and took off after Hobs and Wicked.

Diandra was doing a great job of keeping the Wizard busy, we made it to the trees, unscathed. By the time I was crouching at the edge of the copse, looking dubiously at the remaining land between us and the ridge, Hobs was back from another assessment of the landscape.

He shook his head. "It's pretty open from here, Miss. There's no way to get there without him seeing us."

I bit my lip. If the Mage decided to pummel us with his dangerous magic, we'd be toast within seconds. "There has to be another way..." I murmured to myself.

A massive boom shook the ground, toppling Hobs and me to our backs. Wicked landed on top of me with a soft grunt. For several moments after the explosion, rocks and dirt rained down on us, the pieces so small they literally sounded like rain.

I crawled over to the edge of the trees and peered back to the spot where Diandra had been.

There was a large crater in the ground, black and still smoking.

She was gone. Tears slipped down my face. "Poor Diandra."

Hobs wrapped long fingers over my shoulder. "Miss, we need to keep moving."

I nodded. Taking a deep breath, I looked at my cat. "You have to stay here. It's going to be really dangerous out there."

"Yeowww!" Wicked slapped me on the ankle, claws out. He drew blood and then hissed and growled as if he fully intended to follow up the claws with something even more painful.

"I can't lose you, buddy."

Wicked straightened, his narrow chest beginning to glow the same orange color that flared to life in his eyes. My hearing dulled, the sound of raining rock fading away as Wicked's magic pulsed away from him like sonic waves.

I shook my head, trying to get my ears to pop. But the muffling effect came from Wicked's magic, and it was growing rather than shrinking.

The dull echoes of sound throbbed around us. Trees faded to shadow as if they were covered in gauze, masked from view. When I spoke Wicked's name, my voice sounded inside my head but I got the distinct impression it didn't make it beyond my lips.

Hobs' warm fingers slipped into mine. I looked down into his pale, blue gaze, frowning.

He smiled. Behind him, a hazy tunnel of gray

light opened up, and he tugged me into it. I looked back at Wicked, intending to tell him to stay put, but he was gone. When I turned back to the tunnel, I saw the muted glow of his orange energy dancing along its walls ahead of us.

With a weary sigh, I shook my head and let Hobs tug me into the veiling tunnel my cat had made. When we got home, Wicked was going to get a stern talking to about not listening when I told him to do something.

Yeah, that was going to go well for me.

Wicked's camouflaging tunnel disappeared with a sigh as I stepped out of it. We stood in front of a cave entrance that was much too similar to the one that had trapped Sebille and I before. My fingers clenched under a wave of nerves, my stomach twisting.

But Diandra wouldn't have sent us there if the cave wasn't safe.

Would she?

Hobs shot away and returned almost instantly. "There are a lot of Walts in a barred room back there."

Relief swept through me. "His family." I started forward. "Show me where they are, please?"

The cell was large, nearly the size of the entire living room at the Seer's hut. It was full of Walt's family, their green gazes tight with worry. None of them moved as I approached. "It's okay," I told them. "I'm here to get you out."

They continued to stare as if they hadn't heard me. Grampa Mong blinked suddenly, turning to Walt's parents and saying something I couldn't hear.

I grabbed the door and gave it a shake, looking around for a key. I looked at Gramps since he seemed to be the only one speaking. "Do you know where the key is?"

Gramps smiled and said something to his wife. She laughed.

I couldn't hear any of it.

"Miss?"

I shook my head. "There's probably a muffling spell." I quickly searched the area, finding a large, old-fashioned key resting on a small outcropping of rock across and down a ways from the cell.

"Miss, I don't think..."

I ignored Hobs and slipped the key into the lock. Turning the heavy piece of metal, I yanked on the door and pulled it open. I lifted my head and fixed the Mongs with a smile.

They were gone.

"Miss, I think it was an illusion."

My heart started to pound. *No!*

The room spun violently. I fell forward, my

hands barely catching the edge of the rusted iron door before I slammed into it with my head.

The silence in the place throbbed with active energy, telling me it was manufactured rather than real. A thick, white fog oozed around our feet and rose to pack my ears and nostrils with ozone-scented magic. My head felt like it was stuffed with cotton.

Unable to use any of my senses to asses my surroundings, my mind shifted to looking for internal stimuli, pulling recent memories forward and shoving them through my brain.

Inside my head, the Wizard's deadly energy slammed into us again, and I relived Wicked's near death, the pain of it just as visceral as it had been the first time around.

I watched the Mage's rage-fueled magic attack Kanish, sending her to the ground on a terror-filled roar.

I experienced for a second time, the total annihilation of Diandra, smelling the acrid black smoke that was all that was left of the Seer who was trying to help.

The pain was like razor blades slicing through my gut.

Wicked flying through the air.
Kanish crashing to the ground.
Diandra being blown to pieces.
Wicked flying...
Kanish crashing...

Diandra...?

Diandra...?

Something wasn't right.

Wicked flying...

Diandra...

Where was Diandra? Where was Walt? Where was Walt's family? Where were the other Seers?

My brain hurt as images and questions and impossible outcomes spun through it. The questions dug sharp claws into my mind, unwilling to let go as I tried to shove them aside to clear my thoughts of the constantly shifting images.

I couldn't form a solid thought. There was too much going on in my mind.

My world rolled beneath me.

Explosions ground against my hearing, leaving behind the stench of battle and death.

Voices screamed above the cacophony.

Agony...smoke...destruction...energy spearing upward...Kanish falling...Wicked flying...Diandra...

Diandra...

Diandra!

"Naida! Trolls trousers! Stop rolling around and screaming." A cold hand slapped me across the cheek.

My eyes shot open and I looked up into judgmental green eyes. A bright red curtain of hair fell on either side of the Sprite's long, narrow face, the color drawing the army of freckles out and making them look even more vibrant across her nose.

I sat upright, grasping Sebille's wrists. "I know. Oh my goddess, I know!"

Sebille frowned. "Know what?"

"I know what was wrong with the pictures in my mind."

"Oookayyy," she looked past me at someone, giving whoever it was her patented, "Looney Tunes" look.

"Miss," Hobs said, sounding worried.

I shook my head, shoving to my feet. "It's not the Wizard. I mean, it kinda is. But not really. Nobody's who they said they were and I'm so stupid. I just brought him here and handed him over." I smacked myself on the forehead with my open palm, the pain ripping the last of the muzziness from my brain.

I grabbed Sebille's arm. "Come on. We need to find Walt and his family. They're in terrible danger."

"That's what we're trying to do," she told me, still looking like she was an eye-blink away from an eye-roll.

I nodded. "Yes." I turned to Hobs. "How did you find us before? At the other caves?"

He frowned, his forehead compressing so that the little swatch of hair between his ears touched his raised brows. "We climbed the steps."

"Show me where they are," I told him, giving him a gentle nudge to get him moving.

"Naida, have you lost your mind? That wasn't here. It was at the other place. By the gate."

"I know. But haven't you noticed the stark similarities between the two? I think they're both magical concoctions, and I'm betting everybody's lives right now that, whoever built them both, built them the same for a reason." I turned to Hobs, lifting my brows in expectation.

"This way, Miss."

20

MY LITTLE BAND OF MERRY
INCOMPETENTS

*T*he steps had been chiseled into the rock at the very end of the cave, invisible unless you knew they were there or just happened to stumble across them. I wondered how the hobgoblin had found them the first time, tucking that question away for another time—after we'd saved Walt and his family from the evil pursuing them.

We climbed the steps quickly and emerged into a cold rain like we'd experienced the last time we'd been on that magicked ridge. The water made the rock slick and cloaked the sky in leaden clouds. If the night hadn't already been uncomfortably dark, the storm with its thick bank of clouds would have finished the job.

As it was, Sebille and I had our magics to light our way.

Fire slashed through the darkness, superheating the air in front of us and drying the rain from the slippery rock. I turned to find Kanish draped over the rocky ground, a glow in her magical gaze. "Hey, girl. I'm glad to see you looking better."

She lifted her wings and roared, making me wince. So much for sneaking up on the bad guy.

"Alrighty then. We'll assume they know we're coming."

Sebille winced. "Sorry about that. She's feeling better, and she's more than a little ticked with whoever blew her out of the sky."

"I can't exactly say I blame her."

We took off running along the ridge, the dragon stomping loudly behind us. Each time one of her giant feet landed on the rock, it sounded like thunder and sent small stones and rocks skittering down to the ground below.

I blamed all the noise Kanish was making for my not noticing sooner when the explosions stopped.

I threw a hand up to halt my little band of merry incompetents.

Except for the soft patter of rain on the rock, silence filled the night.

I sent Sebille a meaning-filled look. "Where's Slimy?"

She frowned. "Don't you think it's a strange time to ask about the frog?"

I sighed. "Where is he, Sebille?"

"He's fine. Why? Do you feel an overwhelming need to be peed on?"

"Sebille?" I asked again in a warning voice.

"Pooped on?"

"Sebille!" I growled.

"I'm here!" Slimy said, his voice disembodied and slightly muffled.

Hobs reached into his scarf and tugged the frog free, holding him up in front of my face. I took him from Hobs' hands. "Look around," I instructed the frog in a low voice. "Tell me what you see."

Slimy blinked. He hopped a little in my palm and turned, then hopped again to turn some more. "Darkness. Rain. There's a juicy looking cricket just over there near that rock."

"Focus," I snarled.

"I *am* focusing," he said in a whiny tone. "I'm starving. Do you know how long it's been since I ate something?"

Hobs shot away and back, holding a struggling cricket between two long fingers. With a snap of Slimy's killer tongue, the cricket was no more.

Sebille and I grimaced.

"There's a soft glow down there. Hidden magic."

"Can you read the intent of the magic?" Sebille asked him.

The frog stared into the night with a blank look, his throat working over the unfortunate cricket. "Subterfuge," he finally said. "I'm still hungry."

I looked at Sebille. She chewed on her lip and then nodded. "Kanish and I will do a fly-by and see if we can tell what we're dealing with. You guys wait here."

I opened my mouth to argue, but she was running toward the dragon before I could get a word out. I watched as she leaped gracefully into the air and landed behind the dragon's sleek head. The big creature took three running steps, flapped her enormous wings, and eased gracefully into the sky. Sebille held on as if she'd been riding dragons all her life.

Hobs stared at me. "We're not going to wait here, are we, Miss?"

"Some of us are. You and Wicked and Slimy stay here, wait for Sebille to come back. I'm going to do a little scouting up ahead."

Hobs gave me a little grin that made my stomach twist.

"You need to do as I say, Hobs."

He tucked Slimy back into the scarf and nodded to a spot behind me.

I turned in time to see Wicked trotting along the ridge, heading toward the magical subterfuge. "Crunchy crickets!" I grumbled, taking off after him. Hobs was just a breeze blowing my hair away from my face as he shot past and ahead of me.

"Nobody listens anymore," I groused. Of course,

I'd pointedly ignored Sebille's perfectly good advice and forged ahead.

Stupid Naida. Stupid, stupid Naida.

The rain drove down onto my head, making it hard to see where I was going. A blustery breeze scoured across the wet surface of the rocks, turning it to ice. I fell hard once, then was forced to slow down or risk plunging over the side of the ridge.

I'd lost sight of Wicked, and Hobs never reappeared. I prayed they were safe. My only option was to keep moving forward.

Flames seared the darkness high above. I looked up to see Kanish's massive form cutting through a dense blanket of clouds, which glowed with silver light to form a dramatic backdrop for the dragon's flight.

No energy arrows shot upward to knock her out of the sky. I hoped that was a good sign.

I slowed as muffled sounds came to me through the rain.

Voices. Shrill with fear.

Nope. Apparently, *not* a good sign.

I closed my eyes, tugging my energy forward. It would be a poor weapon against an ancient and powerful Mage, and I couldn't help wishing I had more. I sent my seeking energy into the night and felt a slight tug on it a beat later.

The soft snick of air warned me that I had incoming. To my shock, the sword I'd called to me earlier slipped easily into my hand, the hilt and weight adjusting to fit me. The burlap bag landed at my feet a second later, finally answering my earlier call.

That was a little better.

I arranged the straps of the bag across my body and gripped the sword. Taking a final, deep breath, I stepped forward and the rain stopped.

I was standing in a room with concrete walls and a concrete floor. Around me, eyes wide with fear, Walt's family stood and crouched against the walls, wrists and ankles trapped inside brutal metal rings.

I glanced around and saw no Wizard.

Walt's grandfather looked at the sword I held, his gaze dismissing it to focus on the energy spitting in my palm. "Can you release us with that?"

I hurried over and tugged the chain straight, sending my energy into the sword and hitting the chain with it. The metal bent but didn't break. I hit it again and again. Finally, the chain gave way. He jerked a leg away from the wall. "This one too. Thank the goddess you came. I'm so afraid for Walt."

I glanced quickly around. "Walt? Where is he?"

"Trying to buy us some time," Walt's mother said. Her face was sallow, cheeks sunken, and eyes filled with pain and worry. She held the infant in her arms and had pulled all the other children as close to her as the chains would allow.

"The Mage will kill him," her husband said. "We're the only ones who can save him." He lifted his arm to show me the broken cuff. "I almost had this one off, but my magic won't work until I get the ankle cuff off too."

Spelled manacles. It made sense.

I redoubled my efforts with Grampa Mong's ankle. It was thicker than the wrist manacle and I couldn't break it. I sat back on my heels, thinking.

"The bag, Miss," Hobs said.

I turned to the door, finding the hobgoblin and Wicked standing there. Hobs looked disheveled as if he'd been through a tornado.

But it hadn't affected his thinking. He was right. Rolling my eyes at my own stupidity, I pulled the bag off my shoulder and reached inside, grasping a six-inch-long metal object. I withdrew it, looking down at the key resting across my palm. It consisted of two slender lengths of blackened metal welded to a circle within a circle within a circle, overlaid by a lightning bolt etched in green. Praying it was the right key, I handed it to Hobs. "Can you unlock their cuffs?" I asked.

Using his supernormal speed, he had everyone unlocked a beat later.

Then he sat down on the floor in front of the kids

with the bag, pulling sweets and toys from the endless burlap depths.

I huddled with the parents. "Where's Walt?"

Papa Mong jerked his head toward the nearest window. "He ran to pull the danger away from us. But we heard demons. I fear the Mage is tracking him with them."

Ugh! Not more demons.

I looked each and every one of them in the eyes. "Can you fight?"

The adults shared a look, their gazes filled with rage. "We look forward to it," Papa Mong finally said.

Holding his gaze, I asked, "Wicked, Hobs, can you get the children out of here?"

"I'll take them," a deep voice said from behind me. I whipped around, finding the Seer from the mountain peak. Without thinking, I'd raised the sword and tugged my magic forward.

Mama Mong reached out and stayed my hand. "He's a friend."

Papa Mong looked at the man. "Is everything in place?"

The Seer nodded. "I don't know how you're going to get the Mage inside the circle, though. There's even more power this time than the last."

Grampa Mong frowned. "We have more too, old friend. And this time, we know what we're dealing with."

Beyond the walls of the concrete prison room, a

dragon called high and long. I knew that was my cue to leave. "If my friends and I deal with those demons, can you save Walt and stop the Mage?"

The four elder Mongs shared a quick look, nodded, and then, in a flare of yellow-green light, disappeared from the room.

"Well," I murmured to myself. "Somebody's been practicing."

I suddenly realized I had no idea how to get out of there. I turned to Hobs and my heart warmed, seeing him sitting cross-legged in the midst of the array of Mong kids. I turned and looked at the Seer, whose kindly gaze was green, rather than the terrifying black from before. Without a word, he walked over and touched my forehead with two fingers.

And the concrete prison room spun away.

I landed in a crouch, arms outstretched and clasping the sword artifact in one hand, my magic in the other.

The silvery energy spit and flared into the darkness. The blade of the sword glowed a soft red, the handle warm and reassuring in my fist. Red. The color of battle.

A battle sword.

Sweet!

I lifted my head and looked around, seeing the familiar peaks of the Seer's lair that Walt had brought me to after he'd found me sleeping by the pond.

The air was icy, but the wind was gone. The rain had shifted away as the cold had grown. Down by my feet, a wintry fog swirled, chilling my legs and feet wherever it touched.

The soft, thump, thump thump of oversized wings had me lifting my head, pulse spiking as I held the sword in a defensive position.

The dragon landed gracefully a few yards away, and Sebille leaped off her back. She strode to me. "Five demons surrounding Walt up there, beside a firepit with six-foot-high flames. There's someone watching, but he's in the shadows. The demons are definitely working for him."

I nodded. "I know the place. Walt took me there before we trekked to the border." I glanced toward the dragon. "Can she fight demons?"

Sebille nodded. "She's ready."

I started off toward Kanish, stopping and turning back when Sebille didn't follow. "You coming?"

Her response was a flare of green light. She buzzed toward me, two inches tall with iridescent purple and green wings. In her Sprite form she was fast, hard to target, and deadly. "I have my own wings," Sebille told me. "You take Kanish. Trust her. Now that she knows who the enemy is, she's good at maneuvering around them."

I turned away and ran toward the dragon. I'd like to say I leaped gracefully onto her back, movie style, like Sebille had, but it would be a lie.

I could have used a ladder.

And a boost.

I pretty much clawed, grunted, and scrambled onto her back. Then, when she took off like a shot, I almost fell right off again. It took me a few beats to yank myself upright as she climbed quickly toward the dense gray clouds. I nearly threw up when she spotted our prey and shot like a bullet toward the circle of red-eyed demons surrounding the fire below.

Yeah, Hollywierd wouldn't be knocking on my door to offer me a stunt-double contract any time soon.

21

IT STINKS IN HERE

*K*anish gave a blood-curdling roar as we dove toward the fire-eyed monsters below. They looked up and growled at us, lifting off the ground and shooting in our direction. Before Kanish evened out her flight, her wings beating the air to send us off at speed, I saw the four Mongs pop into place around Walt, where the demons had been.

I took a deep breath as the monsters charged closer, their eyes glowing evil intent into the night. Their mouths were open in a constant growl, showing us the jagged teeth they would use to tear us to pieces if we weren't fast and smart.

The demons were flying upward in formation, but when they came to within several yards of us, they suddenly spread out, taking up positions around and below us. It was only a matter of time before one of them managed to climb to a spot above the dragon. Then we'd be surrounded.

Hold on, a voice said in my mind.

Before I had time to decipher who'd spoken, Kanish slammed her wings backward, creating a hard braking effect that precipitated a violent downward plunge.

A scream escaped my lips and I started to fly off the dragon's back. I grabbed for a slippery spike and tried to grip with my legs, but gravity and wind were not my friend. I slid from my precarious seat on her back, my stomach twisting in terror as the ground grew rapidly closer. Before I completely fell away, the dragon's energy flickered, a smoky scent on the air, and a ring of sparkling magic reached for me and tugged me back down. The soft embrace of her magic locked me into place like a seatbelt.

We hurtled into the demon who'd been flying beneath us, hitting him with a meaty *thump*. As the monster fell, Kanish slammed the spikes of her agile tail into him, sending him to the ground in a death spiral.

We didn't wait for him to hit. The demons we'd left behind when we'd dropped so precipitously, were diving in our direction.

And they looked mad.

Of course, they pretty much always looked mad.

Hold on, the feminine voice told me. I opened my

mouth to object when Kanish went into a vertical spiral, tail and teeth whipping the air as she spun so fast I had to slam my eyes closed to keep from throwing up.

By the time she slowed to a stop, two more demons were plunging toward the ground, bleeding from an array of wounds no doubt caused by her razor-sharp spikes and talons.

She rolled horizontal again, her sides heaving. Warm wetness bathed my thigh. I looked down to find a long gash along her body, just in front of her wing. "Are you okay?" I asked, wishing I had Sebille's healing magic.

I can fly, but there won't be any more acrobatics, she told me in a breathy voice.

A dark shape dropped quickly from the sky. Too quick. I barely had time to get my sword up before the demon hit. He slammed a fist into my arm as I swung. Pain radiated through my arm and it went numb.

The sword fell from my grip and tumbled away. Snarling in rage, the monster grabbed me, wrapping its fingers around my throat and squeezing. The fingers were rough against my skin and felt like steel bands around my throat.

I clawed at his scaly hands, trying to get some air, and my energy flared against his skin, causing him to jerk in surprised pain. Unfortunately, he didn't let go. But his reaction gave me an idea.

Stars danced in front of my gaze. My eyes felt like they were bulging out of my head.

I shoved fear away and focused hard on my energy, finding it coiled in my core and grasping it before I lost my concentration. As soon as I had hold of the magic, I yanked it forward, slammed my hand against the demon's face, and drove a massive dose of energy into his head.

Silvery light blasted from my palm and wrapped around his head, drawing a panicked scream from his throat. His body tensed, the fingers around my throat tightening until something creaked inside my neck.

My throat was collapsing. I could already feel the weakness his destruction was causing in my limbs.

In pure desperation, I pulled everything I had left into my hand and shot him with a final blast of my flagging energy.

It was finally enough.

The monster's fingers let go of my throat and he drifted backward as Kanish shot away, his wings giving two half-hearted beats on the air before they went slack and he plunged toward the ground.

I sucked in a tortured breath, pain screaming through my throat and chest as the air scraped over my damaged throat. My oxygen-starved brain was muzzy. There was something I needed to remember, but I couldn't quite grasp it.

A long, black shape rose above us, red eyes gleaming as the remaining demon reached out and raked its claws along Kanish's exposed side. He surged forward and clamped his teeth onto the dragon's wing, twisting violently to inflict maximum damage.

She screamed, her body falling into a roll as she fought to get free of the demon.

I shook my head in an attempt to clear it and held on tight as Kanish's binding magic slid away. She needed every bit of magic she had to stay in the air and fight the demon.

I knew I needed to do something.

Despite Kanish's efforts, we were falling fast, the ground flying up to meet us.

We had only seconds before we crashed. And it was all I could do to keep my seat.

My energy stores were empty. My sword had dropped goddess knew where, and I couldn't release my grip on the dragon or I'd risk falling.

Then I realized that, either way, I was going to die.

It took me a beat to wrap my mind around that and another beat to accept it.

I did the only thing I could.

I closed my eyes, thanked the Universe for a short but entertaining life, and released my hold on Kanish.

My eyes snapped open, my hands flashed out,

and I grabbed hold of the demon's wing as I fell away.

She released Kanish's wing to scream in agony as my weight stretched the ligaments of her wing. She reared back, slashing at me with her claws as the dragon shot away.

Safe.

I sighed, glad Kanish would live, and wrapped myself around the wing, holding onto it with everything I had.

Agony speared through me as the demon twisted around and raked at me with her claws.

I focused on the ground flying up to meet me, willing myself to tune everything else out.

We were seconds from death when a two-inch-long bug buzzed past and magic sliced, green and deadly, into the demon.

She went limp and I released the wing, letting her fall to the ground before me.

Warm energy spread beneath me and I eased to the hard, cold ground a moment later.

Sebille flashed into full size, eyeing me. "I can't leave you alone for a minute," she complained crankily. "Look how much trouble you've gotten yourself into."

I tried to laugh but it hurt too much. "I've decided I really don't like demons."

"It's just as well. I'm pretty sure they don't like you much either."

She laid her hands on my back and healing warmth infused the torn skin there. Then came the rebuilding energy, which hurt like a giant pimple on date night. Agony bit my skin like a thousand red ants and I bit my tongue against it, determined not to scream.

A small, warm body curled against mine and the pain eased away. I sighed, wrapping myself around Mr. Wicked. "Hey, buddy. Thanks." Then I let myself fall into blissful sleep. m

---

"Miss?"

I was so tired. I swatted at the pesky fingers poking my shoulder. "Go away."

"Miss, I think Miss Sebille needs your help."

I groaned, my back and shoulders stiff from lying on the hard ground. And I was so cold...

Hobs' words finally sank in and sleep fled. My eyes shot open and I sat up too fast, vertigo taking me for a moment. Holding my head, I groaned again. "What happened? Where's Sebille? Where's Wicked?"

"She told me to let you rest," Hobs said, his face clearly displaying how unhappy he was. "But she needs you now."

I shoved to my feet, taking stock of my condition. I had residual stiffness and a dull ache across my back from the healing. I took a shallow breath until it eased. I looked at Hobs. "Where is she?"

He held out a hand and lifted a light brown eyebrow, willing me to take it.

Knowing I'd probably regret it, I did.

My feet left the ground, wind scoured past, and all the air in my lungs whooshed out. We stopped so suddenly my internal organs slammed against the front of my body and my hair fell over my face.

I opened my mouth and sucked in a breath, trembling. "What in the goddess's least favorite shoes just happened?"

"Shhh!" Hobbs held a finger in front of his lips. He pointed past the big rock that was shielding us. "Over there," he whispered.

I peered carefully over the rock. What I saw made my blood run cold.

The Mongs stood in a half-circle around the fire. Walt was free, and he crouched beside the fire, his hands glowing as he chanted with his eyes squeezed shut. Magic swirled in the air around the family, but it stopped just beyond the fire, kept at bay by a wall of magic I couldn't see.

I was pretty sure I knew the source of the wall since the Mage was holding a blood-jeweled athame to Sebille's throat.

Hobs shifted, pulling Slimy from his nest in the Christmas scarf. The hobgoblin placed the frog on top of the rock, where he proceeded to blink and shiver. "The knife is pulling magic from Sebille," he told me. "It's keeping the Seers' magic at bay."

I nodded. "How long have they been at an impasse?"

Hobs shrugged. "Long enough for my toes to just about freeze off."

Given that the hobgoblin had shown little susceptibility to the cold to that point, I figured it had been a while. "What is the Mage trying to do?"

"Right now, I think she's just trying to escape the trap. But she said something about getting rid of the rest of the Seers and owning Plex."

Power and control. Every bad guy in the world wanted either money or power. Or both.

I sighed. "Well, that's not very original, but it explains a lot."

"Do we have a plan?" I asked Hobs.

"I was hoping you'd have one," Hobs whispered.

I thought about it. To my untrained eye, it appeared the Mongs just needed something to tip the scales in their favor. We needed to get Sebille away from the Mage. I glanced at Hobs. "If I distract her, do you think you could grab that knife?"

He nodded enthusiastically.

I thought about it a moment longer. If I simply walked into the clearing, the Mage would know I was trying to distract her. She hadn't gotten where she was without being very clever.

I had an idea. "Hobs, do you still have that bag?"

"It stinks in here," I complained to Hobs.

He was eyeing me with a wide gaze, keeping his distance as I wriggled and shoved at the skin over my shoulders.

The world around me was mottled under a red glow. It was like wearing rose-covered glasses under a cloudy sky. My nostrils flared under the sulfurous stench that permeated the scaly skin covering me. "Are my eyes glowing?"

Hobs' only response was to take a step back.

I took that as a firm, yes. "Okay," I whispered. "Are you ready?"

He swallowed hard, his Adam's Apple bobbing in his skinny throat. Though his eyes looked like they were about to pop out of his head, he nodded.

"Okay, let's do this then."

I reached for his arm. The hobgoblin winced, stepping away. Fear laid claim to his adorable face, making me feel like the monster I was portraying. "It's me, Hobs. I won't hurt you."

He swallowed again, then took a shaky breath and offered me a skinny limb.

I wrapped my scale-covered fingers around the pale offering and gave him a smile.

He went entirely colorless.

Oops! I just showed him my razor-sharp teeth. My bad.

"Sorry," I whispered.

I stepped around the rock and tugged him with me. He stumbled a little as I'd instructed him to do, and I pushed him closer to the woman holding Sebille hostage.

Wilshire Montague a.k.a. Diandra gave me a surprised glance. "What's this?"

I made my voice as deep and gravely as I could. "Prisoner."

She looked at Hobs, who was shivering and pitiful on the ground between us, and I watched her dismiss him as a non-threat.

I almost smiled.

Sebille's gaze was locked on me, watching carefully. I let my eyes widen and gave her a little finger wave where the Mage couldn't see it.

Sebille rolled her eyes.

That made me want to grin. For the good of everybody, I restrained myself. I glanced at the Mongs across the fire. "What's all this?"

It was a mistake to ask a question. I'd known it would be a risk. But my job was to distract the Mage and, short of breaking into a waltz or busting out in song, talking was the only way I knew to do that.

"This is *my* business, Demon. You forget yourself."

I shrugged stepping closer to the Mong end of the circle and earning myself several alarmed glances. I would have tried to look harmless, but that would have really alerted the Mage so I growled at the Seers.

A quick jolt of black energy shot out of the wall and zapped my backside. I yelped and glared at the Mongs.

When I turned around, Wilshire was staring at me, an assessing look in her eyes.

And Hobs was not where I'd left him.

I smiled, showing her my teeth, and saw the moment when she realized the jig was up.

Hobs was a blur on the air, his brightly colored scarf leaving green and red stains on the air as he zoomed past and away.

The Mage looked down at her empty hand, and Sebille turned, placing her glowing palms over Wilshire's face and sending a burst of energy into her mind. The Mage twitched violently and started to sag toward the ground.

A cool breeze announced Hobs' arrival next to me. A pair of blinking black eyes stared over at the Mage from the hobgoblin's scarf.

Sebille was turning toward the Mongs

"Watch out for her," Slimy warned.

I turned back just as Wilshire straightened again, a grim smile on her pretty face, and sent a bolt of black energy toward Sebille.

The Sprite leaped into the air, changing form and skittering away before the energy hit her, but it shot across the clearing and hit the Mongs, exploding into blue-black flames that threw them off their feet.

"No!"

Time slowed as Wilshire started forward, another ball of black energy roiling in her palm. Smoke lay thick upon the area where she'd engaged the attack, and I couldn't see Walt and his family on the other side.

I didn't know if they were safe or dead. But fear was like poison in my belly.

She'd hit them hard.

The smoke split apart and all five Mongs stepped through, their hands outstretched and their eyes pure, glossy black. Their lips were moving in a constant chant, their steps sure. As one, they threw the dust from their hands into the flames of Walt's fire and it flamed into a solid wall of flickering orange and red heat that rolled up to the edges of the circle and flashed around it, enclosing the Seers and the Mage in the circle together. The energy that had divided the circle disintegrated into thick, black smoke and the Mongs walked through it, their forms encompassed by spitting gray strings of energy that danced on the magic-clogged air.

As I watched, the strings snapped out and grabbed the Mage by each wrist, each ankle and around the throat. Every individual strand of magic initiated from a different Mong, and when they tugged, they brought her to the center of the flaming circle, jerked her to her knees, and wrapped her in a dozen glistening strands of magic.

She threw her head back and screamed as the magic did its thing.

"They're pulling the energy out of her," Slimy said, sounding awed.

A moment later, the magic strands turned to ash and dropped to the icy ground. Diandra/Wilshire didn't move. She remained kneeling, head bowed and eyes blankly staring.

The Wilshire Plex Seer walked out of the darkness, stepping over the circle and breaking it.

And the magic fire died in one gasp of smoke-scented air.

22

HOME SWEET HOME

*T*he Mongs blinked, the black fading from their eyes, and looked at each other.

"We did it," Walt said. He grinned, and his family sent up a cheer, clapping him on the back. "We did it," he said again, looking at Wilshire Montague as if he couldn't believe it.

I started forward and he flinched. "Oh, sorry," I told him. I grabbed the demon skin I'd pulled from the burlap sack, tugging it off my head and shoulders. "It's me."

He eyed the collapsed demon head and grinned. "How'd you do that? It looked so real."

"It's a long story," I told him. "But I got the idea from having Skinwalkers crash a party of mine."

Mrs. Mong hugged me, though she grimaced at the demon skin I was still half wearing. "Thank you, Naida. We've been trying to identify Wilshire for decades. But we never imagined it was sweet Dian-dra." She frowned. "She's made it impossible to do our jobs as Seers."

I frowned. "Is that why your family didn't take their places at the gate?"

She nodded. "Though, it's not as you think. We did embrace our responsibilities, but not as controllers of the gate. We've been hiding in plain sight for a century, waiting for the witch to show herself."

"Unfortunately, we believed the fiction about the Wizard," Mr. Mong said. "Diandra did a good job spreading false information. It effectively threw us off her trail."

"So, there never was a Wizard?" Sebille asked.

"Apparently not," Walt responded. "And she obviously didn't fling herself off the ridge."

Despite myself, I was impressed. Diandra had done a pretty effective bit of spell work that had only required writing false histories of the Dark Rages. "But how is it that the Mage didn't know what or who you were all these years?"

Walt lifted his palms and indicated our surroundings. "This is more than the Wilshire Plex Seer's living room. It's a mini-dimension, unknown to the Mage until she came through the portal for the first time. This dimension has cloaked Wilshire Plex in anonymity, hidden our magic." Walt frowned. "I should have known better than to bring

Diandra...Wilshire...here. I endangered everybody. But I believed she was a Seer."

"No, son," his father said. "This reckoning has been a long time coming. It is good we finally met her here."

"How'd she get your whole family?" I asked.

Grandma Mong sighed, "I'm afraid that's my fault. The Mage sent a summons using Gus's workings. He was checking the perimeter as he does every day at this time, ensuring it hadn't been breached. His fire workings were untended. I should have known it wasn't him but I reacted and we all came quickly as the summons requested. Of course, as soon as he felt the violation Gus returned, but it was already too late."

"Who's Gus?" Sebille asked.

The Seer with the watch lifted a hand. "That would be me." We watched Gus collect Wilshire, slapping handcuffs on her wrists that looked like polished ebony. He gave me a nod. "Nice work, Keeper. It's been an honor working with you." Tugging the watch from his pocket, he narrowed his gaze on me. "I believe you might be late for something?" He spun one thick finger over the face of the watch, counterclockwise. "Oh, look at that. Not late at all." He grinned at us before tugging his prisoner to her feet.

I shook my head. "And that gobbledygook you fed me when Walt and I came to visit you?"

He looked offended. "What gobbledygook?" But I was pretty sure I heard him chuckling as he started away, the Mage in tow.

"Wait!" I called out to him.

He stopped, turning back. "That was you on the ladder, wasn't it? At the wrinkle?"

He inclined his head. "Where dimensions cross, bonds are formed, bargains set." He smiled. "We'll meet again, Keeper."

I watched him walk away and sighed. "Gobbledygook.

Walt laughed, drawing a smile from me.

"What about the other Seers?" I asked. "Did they really run away?"

The family shared a smile. "They're in hiding here in Wilshire Plex. Most of them, anyway." She frowned.

Grampa Mong gave her a hug. "We lost a couple in the beginning before we started to recognize the signs."

"Signs?" Sebille asked.

"Yes," Walt said. He looked at me. "That fruit you ate? It's a magical artifact. When it's eaten, it portends if someone is in mortal danger from dark magic. We created the fruit so we'd know when one of us had been targeted. The Wizard, or what we thought was the Wizard, was the most likely source of dark magic in Plex."

"We never told the Seers at the gate what we

were giving them when we brought the weekly portion of fruit. They just believed they were getting a treat," Mama Mong said. "But if the portent showed up in Gus' workings, we knew that person was in danger and we quickly moved them into hiding," she finished.

At least I finally understood why Walt had panicked when he saw that I'd eaten the fruit. "But it's just right out there." I objected. "Anybody could eat it."

Walt laughed. "Not anybody, Keeper. Only someone who knows it's there. Or someone who controls artifacts.

There was a moment of silence, during which the Mongs just grinned at each other. Then Grandpa Mong voiced some of the relief I think they were all feeling. "I can't believe the Mage is finally subdued," he said.

Walt grinned. "We can finally take our real names back."

Then it hit me. "Montague a.k.a. Mong."

They nodded.

"Something's bothering me," Sebille said. "Why didn't you recognize Diandra as Wilshire?"

"She was under deep glamour," Walt explained. "And she was one of the weakest Seers at the gate. Of course, that should have been a clue. But we didn't realize who she was until she brought you through the portal. She shouldn't have known about the portal. Unless she knew how to cast a spell to find it." He eyed me. "A spell that is very volatile."

Another piece of the puzzle slipped into place. "The explosion that burned her."

"Yes. It was genius, really. With her so badly hurt, we all just assumed the Wizard had interfered with her workings that night. But when she heard what happened to you in the caves," Walt began.

"She put two and two together and realized the caves had been protected with a repelling spell. Which meant someone was hiding something in there," Sebille said.

Walt nodded. "With her level of magical ability, it didn't take her long to figure out what we were hiding. And my presence there ensured the portal would open when she focused her magics on opening it."

"But it's all done now," Walt's mother said, giving him a hug. "The Seers can return to the gate, and we can begin training in truth so our children can someday take their places as Seers."

They all looked so pleased that, for a moment, I felt good too. Then I remembered we were trapped in Plex. Maybe forever. I sent Sebille a terrified look. "We totally blew our twenty-four-hour deadline."

Sebille glanced at Walt.

"I think Gus just took care of that," he said. "You should have plenty of time to use the book."

Sebille expelled a relieved sigh. Though I

suspected she might have had extra time built into the Book's timetable. Just because she's Sebille.

We stood just outside the hut as the suns climbed the horizon, turning the sky gorgeous shades of pink, purple, and, strangely, green. Sebille and I gave Walt a hug, extracting a promise from him that he'd come visit us at Croakies sometime soon, and then gathered everyone together for the trip through the book.

I stared at the dragon standing nearby, a hopeful look on her face, and felt a niggle of worry. "We'd better not head to the bookstore," I told Sebille. "I don't want to have to repair the ceiling again."

She looked at Kanish and understanding lit her face. "How about the artifact library?"

That was a good idea. That way the dragon could stay with us until she figured out how to shift back and forth from her two entities and got used to our world. "That works."

Hobs handed Slimy to me.

I looked into the little green squish's face, feeling fear creeping up my spine. What if he stopped talking when we went home again? I'd really gotten used to conversing with the opinionated little guy.

I'd miss his snotty little comments.

Surprising me, the frog plucked the worry from my mind.

"I can only be what I can be," he told me, sounding like Gus the Seer.

"Yeah, thanks for that." I gave him a sly smile. "I'm thinking I can only provide the good crickets if I can provide them."

"Har." He twisted his lips unhappily, but I felt a spark of humor in his mind.

Wait...in his mind?

"Is everybody ready?" Sebille asked.

I waved at Walt. "See you soon?"

He nodded, taking a step back as if afraid he'd be pulled into the book with us.

I looked at Sebille. "I'm ready."

"Everybody needs to be touching."

I clutched Slimy. Wicked jumped into Sebille's arms. She twitched in surprise and glared down at him. He responded by rubbing his head on her chin, making her grimace.

I hid a smile. Things were already getting back to normal.

I reached out and clasped Hobs' hand and he touched Adelaide. We all shifted sideways so Sebille could touch Kanish with one hand.

I opened the book with my mind and pictured the artifact library that was our destination.

The pages started flipping. Flipping. Flipping.

I frowned.

Flipping.

"Sebille?"

Flipping.

Flipping.

The pages finally stopped, and I looked down at a picture of the Croakies artifact library, relief spreading calm through my system. I tucked Slimy into the pocket of my borrowed fleece jacket. Reaching toward the book, I placed my palm over the picture and waited.

The magic grabbed us, yanking us hard before it twisted us like a wet rag and wrung all of our awareness out, ripping the world of Plex away and plunging us into the gray void of the in-between. A heartbeat later, we landed in a tangle of bodies, everyone mashed together and then falling apart as our feet hit the concrete floor of my beloved artifact library.

My ears rang from the journey, my system zinged, and Hobs ripped his hand from mine as soon as we came to awareness. The dragon landed with an "umph!" and skidded across the floor, smacking hard into Hobs.

The little hobgoblin shot into the air from the impact and hit the metal supporting pole in the center of the room with a resounding clang.

He slipped bonelessly down the pole, landing in a puddle wrapped around the pole like a pole-dancing fireman.

We all waited.

Anticipation built.

Then worry niggled.

Hobs' head came up. He seemed to shake himself off. And he shot to his feet and screamed, "Again!"

It was *really* good to be home.

Until the clanging started. Continuous and insistent. And I had no idea what it meant.

Oh well, back to work!

The End

READ MORE ENCHANTING INQUIRIES

If you enjoyed **Milk & Croakies**, you might want to check out the next book in the series. Please enjoy Chapter One of **Croakies Monster**, Book 8 of the *Enchanted Inquiries Paranormal Mysteries* as my gift to you!

***

Ancient Chinese proverb says, give cat mouse and give frog fly, they'll soothe your monsters so you won't die.

Okay, maybe I just made that up. But I'll try anything at this point.

Croakies is suddenly being overrun by monsters. Yeah. Monsters. And I have no clue where they're coming from. Are they tied to something we've done in the past? Do they have anything to do with the strange phone calls I've been getting from a really prickly local author? Most importantly, how are we going to explain to the humans about the appearance of a certain giantnormous blue monster flinging car-sized cookies around? Where did all these squirrel squattin' songbirds come from? And, for the love of the goddess's favorite spanks, why is there ice all over the floor?

Sigh.

The frog and the cat? Yeah, they're really pretty useless on this one. But at least they're living the good life thanks to my tireless efforts to feed, house, and clean up after them and their naughty friend Hobs.

Yay me.

Mega monster boogers! This magic wrangling gig is for the birds. And the frogs. And the cats. And the hobgoblins. And, apparently, for the monsters hiding at Croakies.

CROAKIES MONSTER

Clang, clang, clangggggggggg...

I rubbed my forehead, trying to soothe the perpetual headache caused by the nearly constant clanging of new orders popping up, and reached out a hand to catch the sheet of paper drifting downward from thin air.

I caught the page without looking at it and shoved it to the bottom of the growing pile on top of Shakespeare's desk.

Sebille came up behind me, stuffing another thin stack of orders beneath the one I'd just received.

I sighed wearily.

Clangggggggggg...

Thank goodness Lea had found a way to mute the sound of new orders arriving, or I'd have gone totally batty from the almost unending barrage. It seemed that whatever we'd done during our recent trek to the dimensional buffer Plex had realigned something in the Universe and a backlog of artifact collection orders I hadn't even known existed had come unclogged and were burying me in work.

Clangggggggg...

I made notes on the order I was currently reviewing and added it to a folder of ten retrievals I planned to attempt as soon as I had my breakfast.

Sebille would leave Croakies with another ten orders. With any luck, we'd each get through half of the planned orders for the day.

Then we'd get a few hours of sleep and start all over again.

Clangggggggg...

I fought despair, feeling as if I was going to die buried under a pile of magical artifact orders.

My head shot up at the sound of a high-pitched screech, surprising a small yelp out of me. Hobs slid past, feet spread and arms akimbo as if he were skiing down a mountainside. His blue eyes were wide and alight with pure joy as he slid past me, my cat Mr. Wicked hot on his trail.

I turned in my chair and watched as Hobs lost his balance and, feet sliding around underneath him, toppled sideways and landed hard in Casanova's perverted chair. A beat later, he flinched, flew into the air, and crashed back into the chair with another shriek of joy. "Again!"

Shaking my head, I turned away. I picked up the

folder I'd been filling with orders and stood, stretching my aching muscles. I'd been working almost non-stop, twenty-hour days, trying to get caught up on the backlog of orders. My vision was blurry and my bones were tired and I had a brand-new array of bumps, bruises, and scratches from my efforts.

My gaze slid to the pile of new magical artifacts across the library. Sebille and I had started out organizing them carefully on top of a thirty-foot-long special wooden artifact table that usually stood mostly empty. But as we'd become overwhelmed, we'd quickly fallen into the "smile and pile" method, and the table was looking pretty chaotic at the moment.

"Again!" Hobs yelled as the chair pinched his narrow bottom, and he leaped into the air with a delighted shriek.

Wicked was tucked into a prim sitting position at the bottom of the chair, feet neatly arranged near his fuzzy bottom and tail wrapped tidily around them. His head lifted and lowered each time Hobs made the trip from chair to air and back down again.

I bit down on the desire to scream at the boisterous hobgoblin. It wasn't his fault I was tired and cranky. He was just having a little fun.

I took a step toward the stairs leading to my apartment above Croakies, my mind already on the retrieval jobs ahead. My foot slipped out from under me.

I gave my own little shriek as my feet slid apart, and I went down, arms akimbo and papers sailing out of the folder to fall around me like giant, rectangular snowflakes.

I lay there with my legs splayed in painful splits and groaned as I took stock.

Headache: blazing. Back: aching. Legs: screaming. Arms: shaking.

Yep, all body parts accounted for.

I rolled over and tried to push myself off the ground. My hand slipped over a patch of...ice?

"What in the name of the goddess's Sunday best...?"

I looked up at the sound of clomping footsteps and found Sebille frowning down at me.

"Why are you sprawled all over the floor, Naida?"

Compassion thy name is Sebille.

"I fell. Slipped actually. On this patch of ice."

Sebille narrowed her iridescent green gaze. "What ice?"

"This ice right here..." I ran my hand over the spot where the ice had been, and it was gone. "I swear it was here a minute ago."

Sebille scoffed. "Sure it was. Somebody needs to get more sleep, I think."

She wasn't wrong. I was dead tired.

Shaking my head, I pushed upright. "I'm going to

go take a shower and have a really strong cup or three of tea. We should get going early today, that Groundhog Day alarm clock artifact is set to go off at nine AM." I gathered up the orders I'd dropped. "Some poor derf is about to relive Groundhog Day for about the fiftieth time." I felt his or her pain. In fact, I was starting to feel as if my life at Croakies was its own version of Groundhog Day.

Croakies Day.

Magical Cluster Day.

Clangggggggggg...

Clanging Croakies Cluster Day.

Rinnnnnggggggg...

Well, that was different. My cell phone lit up and I grabbed it, seeing an unknown number on the screen. "Croakies Bookstore," I answered, my attention scattered.

"Hello, is this the proprietress of the bookstore?"

I didn't recognize the voice. It was male and soft-spoken, the speech pattern precise and cultured. I also detected a slight English accent.

"This is Naida Griffith. How can I help you?" I expected the man to ask me if I could order a certain book for him or if I had a specific volume in stock. Those were the usual questions I got from customers. But his response surprised me.

"My name is Archibald Pudsnecker."

He hesitated a moment as if the name should mean something to me. It didn't. So, when it appeared he wasn't going to go on until I responded, I said, "It's a pleasure, Mr. Pudsnecker."

I could almost hear his disgust through the line. "Yes. Well. I'm an author. Recently relocated to Enchanted. And I'm very well-known," he added that last as if chastising me for not knowing him.

"Oh, that's wonderful. What genre do you write?"

Air hissed through the line as if he'd sighed, long and disgusted. "You own a bookstore, Ms. Griffith. I'm surprised you don't know about my books. Perhaps Croakies isn't the best vehicle for my purposes after all."

Another artifact order sifted downward. Without thinking, I reached out and snagged it. "I'm sorry, Mr. Pudsnecker..." I grimaced at the name. I couldn't imagine an author saddling himself with that name if he was trying to gain readership. "I'm in a bit of a crisis right now. If you could come to the point of what you need, I'll..."

"Never mind," he told me shortly, clearly disgusted. The call was severed with brutal efficiency, and I was left listening to dead air.

"Alrighty then," I muttered. Sighing, I headed for the showers. I couldn't control much of my life, but I *could* turn on a very hot shower and scrape off some of the detritus of the previous day.

Clangggggggggg...

I didn't even turn around as another order appeared from thin air and sifted downward. I'd pick up the pile of orders that came in later. When I got back.

Jingle...

I stopped abruptly, realizing that had been a different type of ringing noise than the one I'd been hearing for the last several days. Or the ringing inside my head.

"Can you get that, Sebille?"

Silence.

"Sebille?"

Nothing.

I sighed, turning to head back downstairs. "I'll get it. Don't worry about me. I'll just do everything around here," I murmured crankily.

Stomping through the door dividing the library from the store, I took my bad mood across the bookstore and peered through the window to the person who was standing on my doorstep. The street light behind him cast my visitor in an orb of white light that pushed the dark of a too-early morning to the background.

My pulse picked up, and my eyes went wide.

The man on the other side gazed back at me for a beat and then lifted his dark brows as I continued to stare without opening the door.

I shook off my shock and unlocked the deadbolts, sending my keeper energy into the magical deadbolt that backed up all the physical ones, and pulled the door open just enough to stick my face through the crack.

Detective Wise Grym looked at me, his jaw tight as he noted my lack of manners. My heart pity-patted as I took in the broad shoulders, rock-like square jaw, and thick mass of mahogany brown hair over a well-shaped head.

"Hey," I said to the too-handsome detective, a.k.a. gargoyle.

"Hey," he said back. "Can I come inside?"

I might have grimaced at the request because I saw him flinch, his dark caramel gaze tightening with irritation. "It's business," he clarified.

Like that would make me feel better. Grym and I had been friends. Good friends. Moving toward more than friends. But then I'd discovered that he'd turned me in to the Société of Dire Magic, a regulating and monitoring body for the magical community, not once, but several times, when I'd temporarily lost control of a few magical artifacts.

As a magic-using member of the Enchanted Police Department, it had been his job to fill out those reports.

As my friend and someone who'd fought beside me when powers stronger than either of us threatened our friends and Enchanted, he should have found a way around writing those reports.

That was my opinion. Wrong or right. I was having trouble getting past them to forgive him. I reluctantly stepped back and let the detective come inside Croakies.

He looked around, his gaze going soft as if he were remembering the last time he'd been there. Christmas at Croakies. When we'd all fallen victim to a pair of skinwalkers. It had been a wild ride, but in the end it had turned into one of the best Christmases I'd ever had.

Which wasn't saying all that much since I generally hated the entire last three months of the year. Magically speaking that is. When one deals in rogue magical artifacts, the holidays are generally chaotic, dangerous, and exhausting.

"What's up?" I asked, shoving my hands into the pockets of my fuzzy robe.

He scanned a look over my robe and slippers and grinned.

Sebille had given me the slippers for Christmas. They looked like gray kittens, with perky ears, long whiskers and orange eyes, representing my favorite cat. I grinned down at them. "My Christmas gift from the Sprite."

He laughed. "They look like Wicked. I like them."

"So do I." There was a moment of awkward silence between us. I glanced longingly toward the dividing door, wanting to make my escape upstairs for that hot shower and a boatload of tea. It didn't look like I was going to get that shower any time soon. But I could still have the tea.

"I was just getting ready to make tea. You want some?"

Grym shook his head. "No, thanks. There isn't time..."

Grumbly gargoyle gristle! No tea either. My day was taking a deep dive right into the dumpster.

"I need your help on a case," the detective told me. "I think there's a monster loose in Enchanted."

———

Check out the entire series here: https://samcheever. com/books/#enchanting

ALSO BY SAM CHEEVER

If you enjoyed **Milk & Croakies**, you might also enjoy these other fun mystery series by Sam. To find out more, visit the **BOOKS** page at www.samcheever.com:

Enchanting Inquiries Paranormal Mysteries - **For more fun adventures with Naida, Sebille, Wicked, Slimy, and Hobs!**
Reluctant Familiar Paranormal Mysteries
Yesterday's Paranormal Mysteries
Gainfully Employed Mysteries
Silver Hills Cozy Mysteries
Country Cousin Mysteries

ABOUT THE AUTHOR

USA Today and WSJ Bestselling Author Sam Cheever writes contemporary and paranormal mystery and suspense, creating stories that draw you in and keep you eagerly turning pages. Known for writing great characters, snappy dialogue, and unique and exhilarating stories, Sam is the award-winning author of 80+ books.

To learn more about Sam and her work, visit her at one of her online hotspots:
www.samcheever.com
samcheever@samcheever.com

www.ingramcontent.com/pod-product-compliance
Lightning Source LLC
Chambersburg PA
CBHW060525260626
47161CB00003B/761